SKY ROBERT

A FATED MATES ALIEN ROMANCE

FROM THE UNIVERSE OF TREASURES OF TRILLUME

Broken Books
Kent, WA 98030

First published in the United States of America by Broken Books LLC, 2024
Her Alien Insurgent Copyright © 2024 S.M. McCoy writing as Sky Robert
Version First Edition: ISBN: 978-1-963669-98-5
Cover Design: RavenBorn Cover Design

Don't let the defeat of the past,
or even the chaos of the present,
prevent you from enjoying your life
and pursuing your future.
As Ashley and Gaven would say,
"We have every fucking right to enjoy what we can from
this fucked universe
before we return to the great rock."

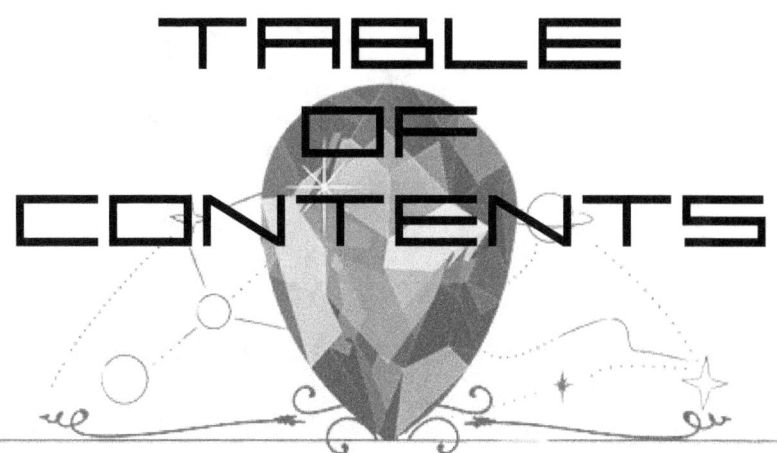

TABLE OF CONTENTS

Trillume Glossary

CONTENT WARNINGS: Her Alien Insurgent contains on-page death, explicit romance scenes, strong language (FMC has a foul mouth, says "fuck" frequently, but not overwhelmingly), a universe-wide fertility crisis, alien culture immersion of a cannibalistic nature, captivity, manipulation, betrayal, slight exhibitionism/voyeurism, and self-harm/recklessness. All smexytimes are consensual, even the dubious consent of not being fully aware of their actions being reality or dream, is still fully consented as each individual may not realize it's real, but both are consenting and wanting said interaction.

If you have not read Her Alien Prince, this continuation of Her Alien Insurgent will have spoilers for that story. Every story is a standalone, you can choose to read this without having read any of the other books, but it is still recommended to read Her Alien Prince first, if you don't want spoiler information from that plotline. You can still go back and read Her Alien Prince after this book, but there are plot reveals that can't be avoided by reading Her Alien Insurgent as it takes place after those events. Universe Plotline so far is provided below for refresher or for those jumping in without having read other books in the universe.

Rushes over to read Her Alien Prince available in Kindle Unlimited: https://books.steviemarie.com/heralienprince

Trillume Universe so far...

A refresher for those who have read other books in the Trillume Universe: *(Spoiler information and Glossary for reference)*

In the universe of Trillume we have a galactic-wide infertility issue created by nano technology that targets species reproductive systems. This technology is called the Ganpan fal, the world destroyer, created by the notorious hacker and outlaw Al-hez, known as the Star Breaker. Humans have created recon teams sent out through the Human Exchange Trade, H.E.T., that use the alien exchange program to hunt for answers and solutions to their fertility crisis. The exchange was created as a means to proliferate human genetics across the universe in hopes that cross-species integration may be the only solution to the continuation of the species with the decline in fertility, but select teams have been infiltrating to find the source of the issue and possibly reverse the nano-tech that has infected reproductive D.N.A.

In the meantime, amidst the crisis there is a power struggle between species and the technology held on the planet Estreldez for the Glorbin Flower, that is a highly efficient and powerful radioactive material that supports advanced space travel. The Ganpan-fal technology has been used as a means of controlling species for the greater control of the universe, by suppressing fertility, and on the planet Krelis, it has nearly destroyed their hive's future with no help from the mentally unstable ruler, Queen Kai.

This is where we find our fated mates in Her Alien Insurgent.

"Small stars fade in eye. Large stars destroy the sky. We break under pressure and electrify." – Al-hez, hidden quote within the hacked coding of the Ganpan-Fal D.N.A. altering nanobugs.

GLOSSARY

Alien Stats:

Estrelds: a community-driven clan on the planet Estreldez that are dependent on radiation from their moons that are absorbed through the many jewels on their skin. Their planet is rather isolated, but for a mating ceremony that they have opened to offworld participation due to the fertility crisis. Their skin coloring has been known to be in many shades of blue, green, purple, and pink. The brightness of their skin, and the quantity of their jewels, called loh, are indicators of strong virility and highly sought after in mates.

They are a species with teeth stronger than rock to grind up minerals as their food source, they do not eat plants or animals for nutrients, they absorb the moon's radiation and eat rocks. Fangs only come out when they are mating or need to provide nutrients to offspring before their teeth grow in by sucking blood from animals and feeding it to their young. Like birds, they do mash up their rocks themselves and then feed to their offspring once they are older, but their teeth are still not prepared to chew their hard foods.

Estreld cocks are stored inside their mating loh, which is a darker jewel plating at their crotch that many offworld species mistake for pant decoration/armor similar to a codpiece. Once mated, an estreld male's cock comes out like a moldable resin and forms to the preferred mating shape needed to pleasure a female into dropping their eggs for fertilization, there is also a secondary smaller cock, used for clitoral stimulation during intercourse (most female estreld's clits are under their mating slit, unlike humans which is at the top, but as an estreld male forms their cock specific to their mate, the placement of the second cock differs.) Often times an estreld cock is segmented similar to having a few knots along their shaft that bulge and swell during mating.

Krelins: a hive-mind warrior species on the planet Krelis that can communicate with their hive through great distances through their horns and allows for unparalleled coordination with their warfleets. They are ruled by a single queen and are usually aggressive by nature, with a history of taking things by force. They have wings, stingers in their forearms, and horns that transmit communication to the hive.

Trills: a poisonous, reptilian species that comes in shades of green (probably where the rumors of little green men from human lore come from) but they are anything but little, and they are an intelligent, strategic conqueror of the known universe who have come into power with alliances across worlds that no one has yet to defy with the necia warriors as their enforcers.

Necias: a warrior species that are known as the enforcers of the Trillume Universe under the direct command of the trill. They have a secondary exoskeleton that comes out like sharp spikes from their shoulders, arms, legs, and back. They are like a walking weapon. (More details about these species are included in the glossary of Her Alien Savior!)

Humans: Within this universe they are part of an exchange program being sent out on cultural exchanges with other planets in exchange for goods and sciences.

Al-hez: the Star Breaker, an outlaw nanobug engineer with a poetic calling card in their DNA splices
"I've been calling Al-Hez the Starbreaker, because every being they touch with their tech lives a broken life." – Ashley

Almder: leader of Estreldez, like a queen but more of a coordinator of many advisory positions of the clan, the position is respected like elders in the community and though she rules, she does not force people to do anything, but guides them and refers to advisors of all specialties for her decisions.

Ashley: human tech wizard of the Starbreaker recon team, curly black hair, brown eyes, hacker

Bel: warrior's cry in krel

Bina: farthest moon of Estreldez

Blackpul algae: sweeter than krel nectar, found on Estreldez

Bryce: blue eyed human anthropologist, part of the Starbreaker recon team

Chester: Human muscle, deep knowledge of Necias culture, part of the Starbreaker recon team

Commander Li-aq: Krelin in cahoots with the missing queen, Queen Kai

Dendil: the tongue/language of Estreldez

Emon: the mother/foster caretaker of the offspring training facility on Estreld

Ganpan-fal: world destroyer (necia) the nanobugs that Princess Klemon created that block reproductive organs

Gaven: Green skin, Chief Tactician of Estreldez, Sky Bender

Gho-ran: Trent's Second in command of the Krelis warfleet

Glilor: reptiles near the waterholes they blinked with a second lid that watched me with curiosity.

Glorbin Flower: Ordin Crystal on Estreldez, a highly condensed fuel source for space travel

Gorn: the jug krel nectar is held

Goddess Lumei: Trill goddess

Goddess of Lenkal: Krelis goddess

Hazel: Head of Security on Estreldez

Helmer Woods: Where the Ki-Hive bar is located on Krelis

Hergslat: an animal that resembles a large rodent with many clawed legs, and tusks, used to help quarry the stones and jewels because their anger made them perfect for smashing the rocks into manageable chunks, and we never had to mistreat the beasts because they were easy to migrate and raging helped them file down their claws.

Hewve lard: Prime import from Krelis to Estreldez (food import)

Huemoons: How estrelds have pronounced humans

Hoomans: How krelin warriors have pronounced humans

H.E.T.: Human Exchange Trade

Kan: the horns of a krelin on their head. In krelin tongue it means to feel or sense

Kansa: fated mate bond of a krelin. "sa" in krel means soul

Ki: the horns that come from a krelin's wrists/stingers

Ki-Hive bar: located in Helmer Woods on Krelis

Kloaph Rite: Krelin mating rights

Klohvin: a bonded friendship between krelin warriors, just as strong as a mate, but more for companionship, but can be more important than a mate depending on the krelin. Many warriors will choose to be bonded to a klohvin they trust and rely on. Being given a mate is often rare and fertile females often take on many warriors, but a klohvin is special. It is possible to be both a klohvin and mate bonded, but usually being called mate refers more to a bonded match capable of fertile offspring.

Kansa: a mythological bond to most krelins as it happens rarely. Klohvin is a bond chosen and can include more than one warrior, though many warriors keep one closer than others. There is no gender requirement to being a klohvin. In fact, many klohvins are MM pairings, and possible FF pairings between infertile females, or even an infertile female with a fertile one that dedicates themselves towards the hive by having many male mates but holds their klohvin above all others.

Larva sack: Kantos sacks for carrying krelin spawnlings

When a krelin warrior bonds with a female to provide a kantos sack for spawn, often times they are unable to provide any other kantos that is not D.N.A. specific to the female they bonded with to create it. To create a kantos is to be fertile for that female alone. A female krelin is able to mate with any male, but a male cannot mate with just any female to create spawnlings. They can have sex, but it would not be fruitful.

Lav sanitation chambers: bathrooms

Loh: jewels that absorb the radiation of the moons on estrelds

Loric: Gaven's closest friend and chief of diplomatic relations on Estreldez, frequently referred to as the Pride of Estreldez

Loretig: flying stone dragon creature of legend on Estreldez blessed by the moon goddess.

Lupa: largest moon on Estreldez, also the name of a moon god of Estreledez lore

Mab: means song in Krel

Mabel: a mating advisor to the leader and future leader of Estreldez, and Gaven's long-standing ideal mate prospect with black hair and green eyes, Gaven offered himself to be sired to her.

MoKre: hybrid species of krelin and human. Gho-ran is a MoKre.

Molt fever: krelin sickness

M.R. Team: Moon Mating Research of Estreldez

Ong: Chief of Krelis Trade

Ordin Crystal: Glorbin Flower on Estreldez

Pan: moon stone, also means heart in Dendil (language of Estreldez)

Rakin: Act of duel between krelins

Queen Kai: Krelis Queen, Trent's mother.

Sired: a tradition among estrelds to bond themselves in service to a mate without expecting to be the primary mate of providing offspring. Many times, estreld males will sire themselves to a female and be whatever the female needs whether that is for physical pleasure or for companionship with the understanding that the female may take on other males or even acquire a mate. A sired male can be anything from a friend that helps raise and care for the female's offspring (whether the offspring is biologically theirs or not) to simply being someone to provide and be a source of physical release and pleasure. A sired male simply wants to dedicate their lives towards whatever their chosen female needs. Often times a sired estreld finds themselves in a situation where they are not fertile and do not wish to prevent their mate from having offspring, or they have fallen for a female that is fertile and a primary breeder for the clan and wish to be given a chance to have offspring with them. There are many reasons to become sired to a mate, and with the approval of the Almder (leader) of the clan, being sired can be both in service and being mate bonded.

Saling: the act of feeling the land through a krelin's kan with the assistance of practiced throat vibrations.

Sotec bitters: Gaven's favorite rock food from Estreldez

Strel: language of the estrelds (renamed by huemoons) to all Estreldez the language is Dendil.

Tarnpul: black rock on Estreldez that is used to absorb the moon's radiation and magnify it.

Trent: Prince of Krelis, Blonde hair, yellow golden eyes, black wings, black horns, black veins of venom, nicknamed: Queen's Revenge, Black Prince

Xol: One of the scientists on the largest Estreldez moon, lead examiner of offworlders

Want to know a little more about where Ashley, our FMC, came from and how she ended up on Krelis? She first appears in Her Alien Savior, Riley's story.

My alien warrior thinks he's supposed to save me, but we may just save each other.

What happens if your exchange program with another alien planet gets hijacked by a warrior that says your contracted host is a criminal? And you're required to help him infiltrate, and apprehend them, or else? Well, I guess that's what happened to me, but it was difficult to know who to trust when being a human meant I was treated like a second-class alien, and injected with nanobug trackers like a criminal.

Dive into a fated mates, spicy monster love romance with instalust, exhibitionism, strong female empowerment, alpha male with consent, and alien extremities. Join the fated mates of the Alien Warriors of Necias Prime in the Treasures of Trillume Universe. All stand-alone romances, within a fun interwoven plot of the universe.

Won PRG's Reader's Choice Awards 2023. Read today on Kindle Unlimited: https://books.steviemarie.com/her-aliensavior

Chapter One

Ashley

Waking up from stasis was never going to be a fun experience when trying to stay under the radar. There would be no medic to ease the ache of my unused muscles, or sleeping through the sharp pain of blood flow returning to my raw skin after a prolonged period of being surrounded by preservation gelatin.

After months of stasis, the first layer of protective skin usually tore, taking layers of dermis with it straight down to muscle and broken blood vessels that were healed during a required anesthesia while a medical team pumped our bodies with nanomeds to heal before we woke.

If I were a more resilient species with scales like the trill or glands with super healing properties like the necia, perhaps

1

stasis wouldn't involve such a painful recovery time without a medbay to assist. But I knew what I was signing up for when I took on a mission to find a notorious outlaw responsible for a universe-wide biothreat that was destroying worlds across the galaxy, including Earth's birthrates.

The pain was expected, but the noise flooding my mind wasn't. Who the fuck was yelling in my ear? I couldn't even process what they were saying through the shouts and incessant clicking.

"Female..." Words were starting to translate through my implant but delayed and choppy, "hooman. Registered name, Riley Spearit."

That wasn't my fucking name.

I might be disorientated, but I knew who I was or wasn't. That was the name of the girl I was supposed to follow so I could find the outlaw Al-Hez. Was she here with me? That would make sense to follow Riley into stasis somewhere. Fucking brain fog after stasis was worse than I imagined, and whatever had happened during that last twenty-four hours before being put in that pod, I didn't remember a thing. Short-term memory didn't survive this method of long-distance space travel.

My eyelids hurt too much to work through that stuck feeling like they were sealed closed with hardened gelatin, and my skin felt clammy.

"Restricted-ed-d." I heard the word echo in the room we were in and needed my translator to start working properly so I could assess the situation I was in. If it was malfunctioning, then I had to pray it didn't reach my keycodes for accessing my hacking programs and my A.I., Indi.

My throat felt like cotton as I made to speak to activate my programs since my arms weren't cooperating.

"Ind-d-di," I croaked, "ac-c-ti-vat-te."

"Ashley, there seems to be a disturbance in my ability to reach my memory stores. I'm afraid I will be unable to initiate any protocols without direct access. If you would connect me to a local server—"

Thank the stars he was still there, but I cut him off before he could start spiraling, "Not imp-port-t-tant. Ass-ssess systems and what's hap-ppening."

Even my fucking teeth ached, and I couldn't feel my tongue. The edges of my mouth cracked with the slight movement of speaking.

"Primary functions show you have been supplied with a standard medpack for stasis recovery, but you have not been given sedatives to keep you stable for this process. There are high levels of metal beyond the standard medbots in your bloodstream, which don't seem to be assisting the issue of toxicity which is interfering with my ability to reach my data stores beyond the implant, and your biomass is elevating core temperature in a natural immune response to foreign particles.

"I fear at this rate, your body will begin rejecting all upgrades to your natural biology in an effort to purge the overdose. This includes my own programming and the likelihood that you will be required to interface with me through the remote servers manually. Protocols to reach out to you will begin after twenty-four Earth hours of not being able to connect."

I groaned. Tell me something I don't know, Indi, I thought with annoyance.

"Your translator should still function without connectivity to other servers. Ah, there we are, your noise control was set to nearly one hundred percent, but the surrounding noise is quite loud. I will try to filter necessary data without harming your fevered sensitivity."

I hated not having Indi connected to his servers. He was so formal and annoying with only the base protocols installed. He'd never know it, because I would never admit it to him, but I liked his personality upgrade that he had downloaded without permission. I was not sure what I had been expecting to happen when I'd programmed him to disregard most laws and rules to hack into places, he shouldn't be but wanting him to be more human wasn't one of them.

"There we are," he said, and then I heard the word, "Sold."

Fuck, that didn't sound good.

"Were you recording?" I prompted Indi.

"I always record, but my data stores are limited without connectivity in your current state. After review, it seems you have taken on the identity of Riley Spearit as a decoy and sent yourself to the planet Estreldez, but the last log pinged to my files was from the planet Krelis.

"You seem to have been redirected from your destination and removed from stasis without proper procedures. You have been sold to a krelin based on recorded conversations since being activated. Ah, you are lucky. They are not transferring you to another ship. This will make it easier for my main servers to find you later. You were sold to a krelin named Domsal in a pleasure district called the Kokova."

Great, I thought sarcastically, just another bump on the road towards finding Al-Hez. Honestly, it seemed too perfect to be hijacked like this, and this whole situation had all the underpinnings of being targeted by the bastard I was hunting.

If he thought being sent to a slut shack was going to stop me and my team from finding him, he had another thing coming. Indi would hack into the system eventually, and I'd be out of there in no time.

I just needed to recover and be ready when Indi's main servers found me.

With a shiver, pain shot through my spine.

"I'm experiencing a series of disruptions to my functionality as your temperature continues to rise." Indi didn't sound "concerned," but that was just a side-effect of only having part of his data available on my implant. There was no point in telling me that there were disruptions when he should be saying which functions were down and actively trying to solve the issue, but

5

I knew when he spoke like that it meant there was nothing he could do. He was worried, not for himself, since this was only a copy of his base programming functions. His main servers would be fine without me.

"I'm reprogramming the nanobots that try to connect with your implant to save the core systems when I'm no longer viable. They are not ideal, but they do as they are programmed within their capabilities."

"She is showing signs of the Fume Fever," someone, not Indi, said, but the voice sounded muffled and distant.

"If she is worthy of the hive, then she will survive," a male hissed, and a series of clicking noises filled the room.

I knew only the basics about the krelins because of their association with the estrelds, but that was Bryce's area of expertise to know about the species we came in contact with. Without Indi or Bryce to help, I was screwed.

"Protocol wizard initiated," Indi chimed, and I knew he'd shut down soon. It was just a reminder that he thought the error that accounted for the infinite improbabilities of one existing in multiple states at once like he explained that he did... I was rambling, and Indi sometimes said things that were hard to understand about himself, but it was clear enough that he believed, given my molecular structure, that I would never fully understand his quantum computing functions but that I would have to believe in the magic of the unexplainable. Though he thought he was perfectly explained, he was a machine that believed in magic. Protocol wizard was a reminder to believe in the small chance of my survival even if I had to tell my mind magic was real.

Magic is real, Indi, I thought with a determination even my mother would've been proud of.

I was going to beat this fever and Indi was going to find me in an alien slut shack. Then we were going to find that mother-fucking asshole that had set us up.

Fuck you, World Destroyer.

Chapter Two
Gaven

Krelis couldn't afford to lose any of their war fleets to the market when King Sylve and his network of outlaws were planning to invade this sector and soon. But with the divide between the hives after the disappearance of Queen Kai, there were more krelin warriors here than I thought there would be.

Commander Gho-ran leaned against the wall near where I hid in plain sight and whispered under his breath, "I thought you might show up, but I wasn't expecting to actually 'see' you."

"No one knows my face," I said with a smirk.

"They still don't, and I don't know if you can tell from the buzz in here, but my hive isn't a bunch of imbeciles. Being manipulated by the fallen queen is different than being unaware. Many are talking about the estreld in the back with a face that looks like green flames and wondering if there is a new psychopath in the sector or if you are the Skybender that has killed many of their hive's warriors because it is a rare trait among your clan to not be sensed by our clan."

He was warning me, but I wasn't trying to hide this time. That wouldn't help me find who I was hunting before he left the orbit of Krelis. Many outlaws were leaving before King Sylve could arrive, but this was the last gathering planned before many of the docked ships were scheduled to leave. This would be the last opportunity for Li-aq, first commander of Queen Kai, to broker a deal off planet.

"I want them to know I'm here," I assured the newly appointed commander of the land-side war preparations. Li-aq was the kind of warrior that would not want a loose end before he departed. Our eyes had locked in those moments before he'd jumped with his queen in his arms. He knew I was the only witness to his even being alive. Mabel believed me, but I could see the doubt in Trent's expression about Queen Kai's being able to survive what he'd done to her. Without Queen Kai, Li-aq was no threat to the hive. But if she lived and Mabel was off planet...

I had to protect her.

It was the last thing I could do before I disappeared for good.

Another krelin walked up to the display and unfurled his wings to show the buyers what they'd be getting.

"Why are you letting them go?" I asked to change the subject as I waited for a good time to give Li-aq the opportunity to attempt killing me before he left.

No one said I had to be bored while I baited my prey.

"They are honorable warriors and know they have done a disservice to the hive that could result in our extinction. They are trading their time for supplies, and many of them know that it increases our chances of survival for fertile krelins to leave the planet, even if it means mating with other species. They are sacrificing themselves for the hive," Gho-ran explained with conviction and belief in his hive. I did not have the same trust in them, but I would not spoil his hope that what they were doing was anything other than cowardice.

They knew, if they stayed on planet or in the war fleets, they would be targeted by their own warriors for supporting the fallen queen when they were not directly manipulated by her will. The hive mind that linked many of the krelins was something I didn't fully understand, but they knew which krelins were brainwashed and which ones followed without coercion, but Gho-ran believed these ones.

"The ones that killed our own to keep her secrets will be hunted. They can't stay hidden for long," Gho-ran said with a gleam in his eye that reminded me it was in their nature to be aggressive. Even one of the good ones like him were not immune to the instinct to purge insurgency in the hive.

"...hooman," the announcer broke through my distracted thoughts. My attention was drawn to the female wrapped up in krelin thread and still coated in dried stasis gelatin clinging to her shiny black mane.

Even Gho-ran pushed off the wall he leaned on to stare at her.

"What is a huemoon doing on Krelis?" I asked out loud, not expecting an answer. There were a few that came to Estreldez for the mating ceremonies, but I wasn't aware of an agreement between her planet and Krelis.

The crowd clicked and buzzed, and I knew they were speaking through their hive bond so outsiders wouldn't overhear.

"Krelis doesn't trade in slavery." Gho-ran took a step back from me as I glared at him. "The hooman has a contract that was verified as transferrable the moment she changed her original exchange with Trillume. According to the trade profile, she was bound for the Mating Ceremony on Estreldez, meaning her contract is open for mating for one Earth year before she has to be returned or stay with her host if she's with spawn."

"Estreldez wasn't her original contract?" I lifted a brow ridge with disbelief that she'd already activated the transfer clause of her contract. Seeing her propped up within her cocoon of krelin thread was grating on my nerves, and if her contract was for Estreldez, then she shouldn't be here, and I'd make sure Krelis kept their trade agreements if she was stolen.

Gho-ran swiped his hand across his forearm, and a document was uploaded to my implant. I quickly scanned her data trail,

11

and my shoulders slumped upon seeing she had already forfeited the original agreement, and Estreldez really was a transfer. Why was I so angry that none of these outlaws were doing anything illegal by purchasing her contract term? Krelis had paid for the trade and was within our trade agreements to resell her contract.

"Sold," I heard them call out, and an older krelin female went to retrieve the huemoon but seemed upset.

"She has fume fever," she argued with irritation.

"If she is worthy of the hive, then she will survive it," the dealer said, dismissive of the concerns.

"What is fume fever?" I asked Gho-ran.

"Your species never had an issue with it. Your radiation is a natural barrier to the excess metal in our atmosphere. When I was a spawn, I almost died from the toxicity of our air. Even krelins don't stay outside the hive for long before returning to the filtered air. The hooman is lucky someone thought quickly to wrap her in the krelin resin after being exposed. Domsal will take good care of her."

"Domsal?"

Gho-ran chuckled nervously, scratching the back of his head. "It's likely Domsal purchased the contract for me. Hoomans don't come by this way often, and I'm likely more compatible with a hooman than a krelin, given that I don't have ki like many warriors."

Understanding dawned on me, and I stared at Gho-ran with new assessment. He was a hybrid. I looked at his forearms. It was rare for a krelin to use implants, which interfered with their kan, and Gho-ran had one in his forearm that usually held a naturally protruding weapon they called ki but estrelds called stingers. He was half huemoon. I've heard their species pronounced different ways, but none of the huemoons I'd observed from the mating ceremony made any corrections on to how we've described their species. Huemoon, or hooman, I was certain it was merely a difference of dialects and didn't concern myself with it.

"And what if she was expecting an estreld?" I pointed out with my arms folded over my chest. Something about the female's mating contract being given to Gho-ran agitated me. She did not know of him, nor could she have been aware of having her contract being transferred before being woken from stasis.

Gho-ran flexed his large wings and smiled. "I've been known to be quite charming, and I learned the language of my spawn maker so she will not struggle communicating with me."

"Why would she struggle speaking with anyone? She should have a basic implant for translation."

"If I didn't know better, I'd say you wished to have her contract for yourself." He laughed at the ridiculousness of that statement. He often joked about things, but I didn't find his words humorous. He didn't realize that I'd been cursed by the goddess and having a mate was not an option, especially not a mate that wished to have offspring.

My lips thinned, and Gho-ran coughed, clearly uncomfortable with the heaviness between us after his words. His eyes turned away to the ground with shame, and it was then that I realized why he was so open with me about his own past about being a hybrid. He knew, and his next words confirmed it. "In the hive, we usually have klohvins. It is a male warrior that devotes himself to another warrior for companionship. Only the queen can activate our mating glands, but there is no reason to be alone waiting for a mate. I never had a klohvin, but I considered my brother the closest I came to having one."

"Are you offering to be a klohvin?" I couldn't help the amusement in my voice despite being irritated with Trent for sharing information about my fertility that was not his to share.

Gho-ran smiled nervously before leaning into whisper, "Domsal doesn't know this, but even with Mabel as our new queen... I am not fertile yet. I guess I have a year to hope this hooman activates my glands, but I knew from a young age that many hybrids are unlikely to have spawnlings without another hybrid to breed with."

Relief made me feel guilty, and I found myself clearing my throat and agreeing to something I wouldn't normally give thought to. "You have poor taste in klohvins."

"You're not so bad," he joked but straightened and gave me a serious expression that would hopefully return us to the stakes at hand. There was a mission to be done and a hive to cleanse of traitors. There was no time for staring at the huemoon that wasn't mine to claim. "I know you knew who I was when we first met, but never turned me into the queen. You didn't even tell your Almder after you saved my life from warriors that tracked me down."

"That's my job," I dismissed.

"No, your job would have been to use me to bargain with the queen. That would have benefited your clan and your Almder. You could have let them kill me, and you wouldn't have had to abandon your spy mission on that vessel. You gave it all up to save me and told no one."

An uncomfortable sensation crawled under my skin at the thought of him knowing too much. It was a split decision to save him, but it was in my best interest to keep a krelin alive that wasn't under the influence of a queen actively trying to invade my planet for our resources. There was no guarantee that turning him into the Almder would have done anything but get us a free shipment of goods and a dead krelin when he was returned to the queen.

"Tactical decision," I excused with a grunt. "Look at you now. You're leading the land forces of Krelis and third from the hive Queen."

"And who's second?" he teased, thinking I would say myself.

"Your brother," I said deadpan.

"And that would make first?"

"The queen herself." I dared him to challenge.

He burst out laughing, and a few outlaws turned to stare at us. We were drawing attention, and he didn't seem to mind one bit. It was awkward being noticed when most of the time I kept to myself.

"You excluded yourself entirely, priceless," he blurted and shook his head in mock disbelief. "You've been my klohvin since the day you saved me, but I'm a patient bastard. I'll wait until you accept me as yours."

"Until you bond with your huemoon mate," I said, not intending it to sound as bitter as it did to my ears.

"Even then. Klohvins are for life even after mating. My mate will have to accept my klohvin is a grumpy hothead."

I should have been insulted, but I merely grinned that a krelin had somehow found out more about me than even Loric, the star warrior of Estreldez and the only one to actively seek out my company, did.

The least serious warrior of the bunch had become a friend on enemy territory.

"Next time you want to pry into my personal life, do it to my face," I warned him.

He scoffed, and his throat clucked. "That mouth of yours is a black hole where secrets go to die. My secrets are safe with you, but it's half the fun trying to find out more about you without you saying a word. I look forward to the day your walls break around me and you call me klohvin."

16

There wasn't a true translation for the word in his language to mine, but I knew the root words meant "blood family" and were closely tied with their Kloaph Mating Rites. They took these bonds seriously, and I knew it was a great honor to hold such a title outside of the hive.

"Since the cycle I spared your life?" I asked with disbelief that he had considered me worthy of more than the title of an assassin.

"Were you planning on killing me?" he asked with amusement.

"It's still an option," I said while pretending to reconsider his life.

"Hate to disappoint you, but there is a line for such an honor. For now, you will have to settle for being my klohvin while you wait."

That reminded me why I was there, and I knew I had to make myself more available for a murder attempt.

"Speaking of which, I should allow my own line an opportunity to give it their best attempt."

"I'll see you at the Kokova then?"

"Prepare a room for my guest," I boasted about the criminal I was sure to catch. The Kokova was a blue-district establishment where Gho-ran had been raised since he was a spawn and where they had cells for unruly guests.

Gho-ran gave me a nod of acknowledgement, and I snuck off as ungracefully as possible without being too obvious that

17

I wished to be caught. Turning around a corner, I released my loh radiation in controlled bursts while pressing myself against the wall. My loh's radiation lapped around me to make my body disappear from the way a krelin's horns could sense object's locations. The heat made me invisible to their eyes, and only a species with heat sensors would be able to notice me.

Waiting for someone to follow in my wake, a krelin slowly came into view, but it wasn't Li-aq.

"You're sure he came this way?" he asked.

An unGor nodded and pointed a wand in my direction. Moon's light... was that a heat sensor? *Sodenmar*, I swore. It was just like being hit in the face with the lazy creature's shit. There was a time in my youth that I was asked to meet past the forest meadows they bathed in and there were a few dangerously close calls.

Li-aq was prepared. Why wouldn't he be?

I pumped out a blast of radiation to burn up the sensors of the device. It wasn't the first time someone had tried to find me with a heat sensor, but they were supposed to be sensitive to heat and that made them vulnerable to breaking if they got oversaturated. It did give away that I was close, which made me vulnerable.

"He's on the move, and he's burned up the detail sensors. All I know is he's close and in that direction."

"You don't know what side he's on?" he snapped at the un-Gor, his throat clucking with irritation.

"You could have implanted heat sensors that are more resilient to radiation, insect, but your kind don't like things that interfere with your horns."

"You could have had the implant yourself," he corrected the disgruntled outlaw. I had to move slowly as I backed away from them to put more space between us. If I moved too fast, they'd be able to spot the blur of my form against the backdrop of the hallway.

"Heat sensor implants make my eyes itch," he complained before adding, "An estreld's radiation isn't the same as most species' body heat signatures. They have to put their own implants inside a tarnpul casing to prevent corrosion, and many can't even get them if they don't have enough radiation to support constant contact with the rock."

"Are you telling me all we had to do was encase the heat sensor in tarnpul?" he growled with displeasure.

"You are a slow insect," the unGor dismissed., "The tarnpul would prevent the device from being able to trace the radiation because it would absorb it before it reached the sensors."

"Whatever, just find him." The krelin turned off down another hall.

Another voice that I recognized whispered behind me, "I don't need a sensor to find you, Skybender."

The heavy weight of a net of tarnpul cast over my shoulders with a shock as the radiation drained from my loh, and I knew he could see me now. I grunted as I strained to stand under the net. There was no point in pushing radiation out when the black tarnpul rocks were adept at absorbing the moon's radiation. All I would do was feed them, while draining myself.

Flying above, Commander Li-aq stared down at me from the ceiling.

"I simply had to wait until the tarnpul in my grip warmed and drop it, since I know you can't move fast while hiding. Surrounded by tarnpul, you no longer can weaponize your loh, and the net prevents you from escaping before my musk can neutralize you. Breathe deep, Skybender. Breathe deep."

I took a deep breath through my nose to spite him with a shit eating grin on my face. I had a filter placed in my nose and kept my lips sealed tightly with the sides upturned with my sense of victory.

Li-aq thought I wouldn't be prepared after being fooled once before. He had caught me off guard coming from the sky in such a small hallway, and the tarnpul net was a nice touch. I hadn't thought to look up, but I should have known the wind from his wings would have been undetectable while I was blasting radiation from my loh. I had been distracted while avoiding the other krelin with the heat sensor, so I wasn't as aware of what was above me. He was smarter than I gave him credit for. His musk wasn't going to knock me out. He was going to have to kill me the old-fashioned way.

Seeing that his musk wasn't working, he swooped to land on me within the heavy netting, but being in the net made of krelin resin and tarnpul was a hindrance to both of us. The netting was woven so close together that it was just as likely to break off his stinger as it was to slip through and impale my flesh. The sharp spikes on his wings were too large to do more than graze the net, and what he was left with was tackling me with his whole weight, sending us both tumbling across the floor with grunts and expletives.

"Try melting me now surrounded by tarnpul, filthy glow worm," he strained to say as we both fought for the advantage.

He shoved the underside of his forearm hard against my face, and I gasped for air as my nose crunched with the blow. Tarnpul scraped across my cheeks as I tried to move out from the netting and his hold.

I sucked one of the rocks into my mouth and ground down on it with my back teeth. Tarnpul wasn't especially flavorful. It wasn't exactly full of any nutrients either, but it did pack a punch for a burst of radiation absorption. My Almder would be ashamed to see tarnpul wasted in this way, but I wasn't in a position to be picky, and what did I care if I cracked a loh if it meant taking this sycophant down? My loh burned with the sudden surge of tarnpul, and I quickly used that time to mold my arm loh into a scythe to cut through the resin holding the net together. Tarnpul tumbled across the ground as I burned through the resin before the tarnpul could absorb the radiation surge. I was gaining ground, and Li-aq could see it as his eyes widened before pain lanced through my back shoulder.

The shock on his face quickly turned to smug victory as I turned to see the other krelin from before had returned with the unGor, and I was outnumbered.

"Don't worry, glow worm. When I kill you, it will be in front of the whole hive for the lives you've taken. You'll live long enough to pay for your crimes."

His musk blew in my face again, but this time my nose was bleeding, and I was forced to inhale. But not before goading him one last time. "I was going to say the same to you."

My vision blurred as the musk took hold, but I watched as his eyes followed mine, and I smiled as I pulled my curved loh back towards myself and speared him through his gut where his scaled skin didn't protect him.

While others practiced forming their loh into spears that could only stab in one direction, I was honing my ability to form a curved blade. Why have a weapon that was only good in close combat, they had asked? It took time and effort to become comfortable with focusing our loh shape along our arms. Many never could master it, and the ones that did preferred something that couldn't be so easily turned on themselves. I knew my entire arm was a weapon that could cut with this shape, and when I "missed" a punch, the blade was pointed toward myself ... but it pierced my target more often than not.

I watched as his blood spilled from his mouth, proving I had punctured one of his lungs. The krelins relied too heavily on their wings protecting their backs, and very few used a weapon shape like mine. The mockery faded from his face, and I grunted as my knees gave out beneath me.

As my vision faded and the clucking noise from Li-aq's throat silenced, I had no regrets. This was what I wanted, if I was being honest with myself.

One final victory, taking out the biggest threat against Mabel and my planet before taking my leave of this universe. I wanted Li-aq to end me while I ended in mutually assured destruction. Why else had I let Gho-ran leave without having backup for myself. He thought I could handle it, and I had given Li-aq plenty of opportunity to have an advantage.

This was the way it was meant to be, I thought morbidly. I had no desire to return to Estreldez, not after what the Almder did to Mabel. I had no desire to be an advisor to Mabel after her rejection of my desire to be sired to her. And with the loss of my previous mate and spawnling, it was too much to carry any longer.

I could finally let go.

I smiled to myself thinking of the gift Gho-ran had given me before the end. I guess I got to have a friend in my final moments, and I let the darkness take me.

Chapter Three

Ashley

A groan tore itself from my scratchy throat, and my mother's shrill voice haunted me as it echoed in my mind, "You think you know everything, do you? Want to do it your way, fine."

I snapped back without seeing the disappointment on her face. "Your way isn't the only way to scratch my ass."

Heat burned my cheeks and down my neck as if she had slapped the filth from my mouth and embedded her own dose of reality check that assured, if I spoke out of line again, I wouldn't feel my teeth for a week after she was done with shoving a bar of soap in my mouth.

Eyes wide, I tossed my head to the side to avoid the large hunk of waxy charcoal she was going to make me gag on until my jaw hurt. Some part of me knew this wasn't real, that this was all in my mind, but I couldn't stop myself from seeing her hovering over me.

"She doesn't actually need us to scratch her ass, does she?" a male voice asked humorously.

"Don't be crass, Gho-ran. It is the fever, nothing more. This isn't something to joke about. Hold her head so she can take the nectar to help her fight for her life," a female scolded, but it definitely wasn't my mother.

Clucking sounds filled the room, and then the soap bar appeared in front of my eyes again.

"No, no, no," I repeated while trying to move away, but my body refused to answer my commands.

"Gho-ran," the woman snapped to get his attention and made me keenly aware that this was not a dream, but I couldn't see them past my mother coming to hold my head down to force a hard bar of soap down my throat.

"You brought this on yourself," she said with pure disappointment before she sighed and took another step forward. I shivered and found my arms were trapped at my sides.

With a determined grunt, I shifted my shoulders back and forth until I rolled over, but I didn't fall off a bed like I thought I might.

I rolled on top of something hard yet warm with a masculine groan attached to it. A green glow filtered through my vision as I squinted, and a pair of bright green eyes stared at me through the haze. My imagination was running wild as my nose brushed against his, and my breath mingled with the warmth of a stranger. His skin sparkled in the dim light around us as we stared at each other in a state of suspended shock.

Licking my dry lips elicited a growl that rumbled through his chest, and my thick black curls fell around us. My heart hammered so hard and my bones ached. An awareness tingled through to the tips of my fingers down to my toes, but something was wrapped around me, preventing me from moving.

We said nothing, and the voice of my mother didn't interrupt again. A new quiver rushed down my neck as our noses rubbed and our mouths lingered closer, yet out of reach. It must have only been moments, but it felt like several minutes passed between us before my mother gripped my shoulder and rolled me back. Even in her grave she tried to control my dreams.

A hand pressed on my forehead as the soap melted into my mouth as I gagged on the thick liquid. It burned down my throat and was sweet like honey mixed with some kind of metallic spice.

"You must drink to help flush out the toxins," she said, but it wasn't my mother's voice.

"How did you find me?" I grumbled. I hadn't spoken to my mother in years, not since she had turned me into the feds. She'd pull out her own hair if she knew she was the reason I met the Black Ops that led to hunting down the outlaw Al-Hez.

"There is nothing we can do but wait now." Her voice was disembodied, floating around me.

A male voice replied, "My kan ache for the first time since they've grown. I can't lose them."

"A kan knows when they are close to a bond. That is a good sign that you are compatible with a mate," she said in a soothing, understanding tone. "It will be some time before the fever breaks. I will watch over them while you go prepare our ground fleets for war."

"I've posted extra warriors around the Kokova. The traitor who did this to him is still out there. I should have gone with him."

"You're lucky you returned when you did. Go protect the hive, Gho-ran. I'll be here," she assured.

"Thank you," he said with exhaustion.

All I could think about was the warmth of the breath on my lips as I stared into the bright green eyes of a sculpted face with a fresh scar across his cheek that was a darker shade of green than the rest of him. I tried to roll again to see if it was all in my imagination.

"Save that energy for the real fight, sweet little daughter." Her hand gently rotated me back and then cupped my cheek. It wasn't my mother that stared back at me through the blurred image. She had round yellow eyes, white straight hair, braided and pinned up with a black carved rod. Black nodules lined from her hairline down the bridge of her nose.

I groaned, and she cooed with soft clucks from her throat in a musical rhythm. "You have much to live for. Gho-ran is destined to spawn the next generation, the future of our hive and the true queen of the hive. Your spawn will be royalty. Krelis will once again have more than one hive queen. It is as the goddess foretold many generations ago.

"A dark star will fall to our lands, burning with our toxic air. She will purge the sickness, and from her union a new hive will bring great victory that will spread across the galaxy. Great things are in your future, and you must purge this sickness to fulfill your duty to the hive."

Nothing was more dangerous than a society desperate for survival and filled with faithful prophecy. If she thought I was some kind of bringer of a new brood of aliens that would set their hive free of troubles, then it was even more urgent to get off this planet and fast. She wouldn't be the only one who thought that way, and the longer I stayed the more time they had to see "signs" that I was a sacred incubator of prophecy.

Fuck, I thought and tried to speak but couldn't do more than groan.

"Shhh," she soothed, "Queen Mother of the MoKre Hive."

MoKre?

Chapter Four

Gaven

For a brief time, I thought I saw the goddess herself watching over me as I returned to the rock from which I came. In a dream, she came to me, and I was held back by the hardened krelin resin surrounding my body. My loh burned until the resin melted from my shoulders, finally allowing me to reach out to hold her in my arms before she rolled away.

She said nothing as the resin around her dripped from her smooth skin. I winced as her hands traced over my cracked loh, and her jaw tightened before blushed lips trembled for me. The goddess couldn't decide whether to be angry at me for failing her or torn that her creation was damaged. I smiled at the blessing to be granted her tears. Perhaps this was the forgiveness the elders spoke of before our lives were returned to the rock.

My Loh warmed at her touch, and her delicate hand was drawn back so as to not harm me again, but for every part of her body that touched mine, I felt myself growing stronger. I reached for her hand and placed it back on my broken loh and sighed with the relaxation of my muscles beneath her fingers. This was what it felt like to be healed by the moon goddess herself. When a warrior was placed at the sands of Lumei's mountain to feed the rock of life, this was why they smiled even in death. They were embraced by the goddess, and their deeds judged upon her altar. Was this how Bina had felt when she guided our daughter to the rock of life?

"Do you forgive me?" I asked, hoping the goddess would take the message to my mate and our offspring beyond this life.

Her dark brow furrowed before she took my head in her hands and shook her own with a kind of sweet sympathy for attempting absolution at the hour of my death. My heart dropped as if it had nothing to tether the useless organ to my body any longer. This was the moment all sense of the universe and stars around me would fade, and my goddess would reject me from the honor of joining my daughter and mate. I was not worthy of being with them when I could not protect them.

Soft lips pressed to mine, and I could taste the salt of her damp tears. All thoughts of my guilt vanished, quickly re-placed with greed and hunger. If she would not forgive me, then I would accept the comfort she offered, and I deepened the kiss.

"We should separate them," the sound of the old krelin, Domsal, tutted from somewhere in the room.

"He is my klohvin, I won't deny him this. We will leave," Gho-ran's commanding voice echoed, and yet it was as if the words themselves were distant and of no consequence. My arms wrapped around my goddess with more possession, and she mewled as my tongue pressed at the seam of her mouth to enter. She sucked my lip instead, and it was her tongue that sparred with me in turn as the voices chattered as if they were disembodied moon spirits.

"She is your mate," Domsal huffed. "It is prophecy."

"Did you not see the way his fangs extended when we tried to separate them the first time? Estrelds only use them for marking their mates and feeding offspring. They don't even come out when they are defending themselves in battle. The hooman isn't my mate," he explained with exhaustion, but the only thing that mattered was feeling my aching fangs scrape the inside of her lower lip and consuming the goddess with my growing need. My cock pushed at my mating seam, begging for her to give me her blessing to release it.

"She is the black star that will lead us to the great hives..."

"Then I'm destined to be a second mate, not the first, and there is no better warrior to be bonded with."

"I hope you know what you're doing; the hive depends on your success," she scolded.

31

"He won't keep her. He thinks he doesn't lose anything if he doesn't claim anything, his very own self-made curse, just as mine is to feel the truth that others deny. Let them fuck tonight, and I can reason with him about sharing her for the survival of Krelis tomorrow."

The words rang clearly in my mind, but as soon as they were said, it was as if they simply vanished as soon as they appeared. I tried to hang on to what was said to process them and react, but the only reaction I had was to the heat of the body against mine. The way her curves molded to my own, it was as if every touch between us only ignited an insatiable desire to have more.

The only voice that mattered was hers as she moaned. Her hands gripped around my neck and pulled her body firmly against my own. The wet folds of her mating loh were already exposed, sliding across my cock seam, begging for friction. Moon Goddess, she was everything a dream was made of, and she was mine before my final departure from this realm. My fingers slid down to feel her, seeking out the vibration of her mating nerve, but there was nothing where the pleasure center should be. Then I flicked up through her throbbing heat to find a hardened cartilage that made her hips buck and thrust all at the same time.

I grinned into her lips, and my uncertainty evaporated as my thumb circled and explored and then plunged my fingers through her mating loh to feel her squeeze around me with a moan. Our heated lips muffled the wonderful sound of her pleasure as it vibrated through my own throat and straight down to the ache in my cock. I'd sought solace in the pleasure of infertile females who simply wished to use my cock to pass the time before they chose a mate, but I'd never felt this kind of need. It was as if I might truly die if she did not have me.

The idea of this goddess using me to pass the time was making my heart hammer in my chest, and a sudden jealous anger surged to the surface. My hands became rough, my lips more possessive, and my cock strained with the need to fill her and push from my mating seam, but I wanted it to be perfect for her. My fingers curved and stroked inside of her as she rocked her hips to the rhythm of her breathy whimpers.

"Fuck me," she demanded, and my anger morphed into something more primal, unable to resist her call.

I pushed a third finger into her mating slit and fucked her faster as my thumb kept rubbing up and down with each thrust over that lovely bundle of nerves that had her squirming on my hand until she shattered. Her walls pulsed around my fingers, and she panted with her forehead pressed to my own. With her release on my fingers, I lifted them to my mouth as she watched my tongue lick each one clean.

Finally, my cock seam heated and released my mating loh which had finished preparing itself for her. I knew I was dreaming in that moment, because it wasn't possible to reform my mating loh without a mate. My cock was permanently formed for Bina the first time I claimed her, and it would forever be in that shape for her and whoever I took pleasure with to pass the time and ease my weary soul. When I fucked another female, it was still with the mating cock I held for her, even after her passing. I was one of the few estreld males with a released mating cock, and many females would seek out my bed, but this was how I knew I was dead, and this was a dream.

The mating cock that pushed from my seam was not one I recognized as we both stared down at it. It curved and held an extra cock head above to stimulate the pleasure center which I'd found located above the goddess's mating seam and segmented in bulges that tapered towards the head and appeared too large to mate with. All I could think was this was what the goddess wanted from me before she returned me to the life rock, and regardless of my lack of familiarity with my new mating cock, it sought out the comfort between her legs as it twitched up her thigh.

"Is this what you want, Goddess?" I demanded as I reached around her gorgeous ass and prodded a finger at her mating entrance once more while my cock slid between her folds. My heart was suspended, waiting to end myself within her embrace. I was ready to claim everything she'd give me and accept whatever cursed afterlife would await me when this dream faded. The head of my cock notched at her entrance as my second finger pushed in a little farther, and I spread my fingers to help stretch her in preparation. My fingers practically pulsated with the heat coming from her slick pussy, and I nipped at her mouth, needing to taste her but unable to pry myself apart. I needed to be closer. I needed to be inside her.

Her small soft hand caressed down my back until she reached between us and gripped the base of my cock, making me hiss with sharp pleasure. With her forehead pressed to mine, she captured me with her brown eyes, and as she wiggled to adjust herself, my fingers released from her reluctantly.

"Make me forget," she whispered in my ear, and I felt like she truly understood what she did to me.

We would forget together, Goddess. Then she guided my cock past the head before her walls clamped down around me, and she moaned. I grinned through the radiating pleasure of even the tip of my cock being massaged by her pulsing need. Her hand flew up to her black curls, and I rotated her beneath me to get better leverage with my hips. I pulled out and felt the suction around my cockhead as I pushed in to stretch her and sink in deeper, but still her walls closed around me, stopping my progress but not impeding her pleasure. I pulsed in and out with just my head, reveling in the way she squirmed beneath me, and her legs wrapped themselves around my waist. Her heels dug into my ass, pulling me towards her, needing more of me, just as I needed more of her.

Cradling her face in my palm, I lost myself in her sparkling brown eyes. Her walls relaxed around me for my thrust to settle the next segment of my cock inside. I bit my lip to stifle a moan while telling her, "That's it, Goddess." I confessed my soaring pleasure as my damaged loh mended enough to fill the room with a soft green glow.

Her back arched, and her fingers yanked from her own tresses to grab at my back. Small nails dug into my flesh, and I preened as if I had come back home to tell my clan I had saved them from war itself and granted them the heavens of the moon goddess. Inch by inch, my cock seated itself within her. My thrusts were slow, working her open for me, and as my second cock head slipped up to feel the divine pulses of her clit's pleasure, I paused in suspended disbelief.

"Moons," I rasped, "you're killing me." She shifted her hips to jolt me back into my body, and I growled.

"Don't stop," she panted. Those brown eyes closed as her head bent back and her heels dug in for the ride.

As if possessed by the instinct of the ancients, I gripped her hips, and with her delicious heat coating my cock, I thrust into her. The responding sounds coming from her invigorated me further, and I held her firm as I pounded against her quivering flesh. My second cock vibrated with the movement, and a shiver ran down the back of my legs from how sensitive it was each time it came in contact with that hardened clit above her mating heat.

I growled, "You take me so well, Goddess." She whimpered as her delicate nails dug into my lower back, and I could feel my own release rising to meet her own.

"Oh god, oh god, oh god—" she chanted, and in her embrace, I felt like one. Her walls clamped around me, spasming, and muscles tensed as liquid heat coated my cock, my own release surging through my very bones and heating my loh. Hunched over her, one of my fangs cut her neck behind her ear, and I licked up the drop of blood to forever have a piece of her with me. I pulled back, panting, as I stared into her brown, dazed eyes. She watched me with a fascination and awe that I wished to hang on to for as long as possible.

"I wish to never wake," I told her. Let me stay here with her, I thought with such conviction that if I believed in it hard enough that this would be real. But if this were a test to see if I had learned my lesson from failing my mate and offspring... then I had failed twice over. The twisted estreld that I was, I would do it again if she'd let me.

"Then don't," she encouraged before her mouth captured my own.

If this was death, I would die a thousand times.

Though my cock was swollen inside her, I moved with shallow pulses. I reveled in the feeling of being so deep within her and those divine gasps and moans as she ground herself against my second cock head until she shivered and bit down on my lip. For the first time in many moons, I didn't feel like what I'd done was a weakness of wishing to give of myself as I had once done with my mate to a female that wished only to keep our actions secret. It felt like returning to a home I'd never had before. She shuddered below me once more, and whatever that word was she used to help release her pleasure gave me a great sense of satisfaction.

"Fuck," she repeated again with a breathy moan.

I grinned like a fool and nipped at her neck before my knot's swelling eased enough to slowly return my cock back within my mating loh, but I did not wish to move. Carefully, I pushed a black curl away from her brown eyes and watched her with fascination. With my head clearing, I wondered why I had chosen to see the moon goddess with similar features to the huemoon I'd seen at the trading post in Krelis' orbit. Was I so jealous of Gho-ran before I died that I would have my final moments stealing his mate?

My brow furrowed before I leaned down and kissed the temple of her beautiful dark skin. Did it matter how attracted I was to someone else's mate if I was dead, and these were my last dreams before returning to the life rock? I held her close to me, burrowing my face into her curls, as if that would allow me to keep this moment longer.

Her own hands pulled around my neck and clung tightly as she whispered, "You feel real."

"So do you," I replied.

"Even the cute way that your nose looks a little crooked like it didn't quite heal right from being broken," she said in an oddly specific manner, referencing an injury I had recently sustained while fighting Li-aq. I pulled back to stare at her with confusion

38

before finally tearing my eyes away from her to glance around the room. We were in a hive, lying in krelin residue?

"Goddess..." I said in shocked realization and as I heard the buzz of krelin wings behind us.

"It's Ashley," she corrected, and then I felt a cold sting lance through my skull, making my temples throb.

The sudden pollen floating in front of my eyes was how I knew it was too late. If I had questioned how visceral she had felt sooner, would I have pried myself away in time to save us both? My nose burned, and my throat itched as the krelin musk hit me. Holding her in my arms, I stared into those wide brown eyes as I tried to wrap my head around being alive and assured her that whatever happened, "I will find you."

I felt my side get crunched with someone's boot, forcing me to fall to the side and off of my goddess. The weight of her in my arms vanished, and an echo of clucking sounds vibrated through the room.

A rough male's voice hissed, "Commander Li-aq sends his regards for finding the Queen Mother, glow worm. We'll be taking it from here now, and as long as you are on the last ship off planet, he won't have to publicly execute you."

I clutched at my head with a growl as his words echoed in my ear as if I were hearing it on a delayed transmission, the crackle of static from the metallic interference of the Krelis air quality. That shouldn't have been an issue with the filtration of the hive, but as my vision focused, I watched as the goddess I had seen in my dreams was haphazardly carried by her waist like a rucksack by his hip. Her delicate arms hung loose beside her black hair, dangling from his hold. Only traces of resin remained on her skin in awkward resolidified clumps that barely hid her shapely curves that had once been in my arms, pressed against my own skin. My breathing quickened as I realized what was happening.

This was not a dream.

I was very much alive.

And that was the huemoon meant to be Gho-ran's mate being taken while I was still weak and disoriented. I fumbled across the raised platform. My knees gave beneath me as I fell hard against the stone ground. The krelin musk was effective in destabilizing me, and I scrambled to reach them. They were already beyond the thin membrane of the living hive door as if it breathed in and out.

Crashing through the membrane that separated this room from the rest of the hive, I clawed at the ground to keep moving, keep following, and catch them. I rushed on unstable legs through the hall as the wings of the krelins blew wind behind them, gaining more ground between us. Clucking throats clattered and echoed in my mind as I roared to push myself through the haze surrounding my vision before the very ground beneath me vanished.

I had rushed through the hive, focused on tracking the flying krelins through the hall, only to miss the drop as they ascended higher and higher. I fell with a pained grunt down a level.

Should I be thankful that I hadn't fallen through a deeper channel of the hive? Or should I be cursing myself for not being in my right mind enough to climb the hive and continue the chase?

I watched as those black curls blurred and her strange, yet soft, brown fingers seemed to reach out for me as she flew farther away.

It took all of my strength to form a basic grapple hook with my forearm loh and dig it into the flexible membrane lining the hive tunnel and anchoring into the hardened hewve lard to climb my way up. This was one of the passages only krelins with wings could access, meaning whatever was up that way wasn't supposed to be available to the females of the hive. Many krelin females molted their wings before they were even mating age, and their wings were not strong enough to carry their own weight if they kept them after their youth.

My arms quaked with the effort of lifting myself one hook at a time, until I reached the top of the tunnel and collapsed at the entrance to another hall, ripping through another membrane separating the hall from the drop down.

Where was she?

Where was my mate? I shook my confused head and corrected myself, Gho-ran's mate...

She would lead me to Li-aq, and I could end this. Find her, kill Li-aq, and finally return to the moons.

41

Chapter Five

Ashley

What a weird fucking dream. His eyes were so sad as he stared at me, almost pleading with me to forgive him for whatever sins he had committed in his life. I wanted to tell him that wasn't something I could give him. Forgiveness wasn't something anyone could offer him; it was something we gave ourselves.

We only had ourselves to rely on.

Then I opened my eyes after the best damned dreamgasm of my life, and he was gone. Well, I guess that was to be expected of a dream, but it had felt so real towards the end.

I groaned, and a gentle hand squeezed mine. A clucking sound echoed in the room as I squinted through the low light filtering around me.

"Do not be frightened," a deep voice said softly. "You have pulled through the Fume Fever and must recover." He was speaking in Trillix, the universal tongue.

He had golden eyes similar to the woman I remembered seeing before, but he also had large black horns and black nodes going down his neck that flexed as he breathed. With a gentleness he patted my hand and then reached for a bowl and pulled out a strange pink bug from the liquid and squeezed it until it gushed into an orange goo that he rubbed onto my skin before I could snatch my arm away to avoid it.

"What the fuck?" I snapped.

"I will not be mating with you while your body must focus on healing. We can discuss mating if you wish another time. I know that your contract specified mating, but unlike an estreld," his voice turned sharp on the mention, before he forced calm again; "krelins do prefer to mate after proving our strength and skill with a series of ceremonies."

What was he yapping on about? I had no intention of mating anyone, I thought with a scowl before I blushed with how hot that dream had been. I mean, fucking and mating were too different things, I assured myself, but who was he to tell me what I wanted? I was about to tell him as much when I remembered Indi had said something about how I had assumed a different identity before going into stasis. So whatever was in her file was what they saw when they scanned me. It made sense. If I was going to Estreldez, they only accepted offworlders if they were participating in a mating ceremony, so I would have had to say I was going to mate if I was going to get past their security checks.

"The only mating ceremony I agreed to was on Estreldez, and they said females controlled who they mated with," I replied with more conviction than I felt. I was guessing what my file said at this point.

"I agree," he said easily, taking me off guard, and I sputtered, at a loss for words so soon after waking up from the worst hangover fever of my life. The only good feeling I had in my body right now was a delicious aftershock of my clit throbbing from what I'd call the most lucid wet dream. "That's why I recovered you from the Kokova before they sold your mating to the highest bidder."

I had heard the word sold when I was fevered and Indi told me about a blue-district slut shack called the Kokova, so what he was talking about seemed to check out so far.

"What's in it for you?" I asked with suspicion, and he reached in for another strange larva bug that he squished in his fingers to mush on my skin. "And what is that bug?"

"The bug is a parasite found in the stomach fluid of a guant beast; they are excellent for detoxing by absorbing into the flesh and preventing the absorption of toxins. It will help your body adjust to the metal in air, preventing an overdose, though the hive helps filter the air to safer levels.

"Oh," I said with a grumble but still wasn't excited about slathering bug guts on my skin. "Well, then when do I get to return to Estreldez?"

"As soon as we can secure passage on a ship cleared to leave. Many of the warships are required to stay close to Krelis, and the ones leaving are headed the opposite direction. We'll have to wait for a trade vessel to return or risk boarding an outlaw ship."

"I'm guessing an outlaw ship would simply ignore whatever deal was made and head the opposite direction of an incoming war." I feigned concern about boarding an outlaw vessel. Whether I could trust this krelin or not didn't matter. I wasn't going to tell him my plans, which was to find a way to get connected with Indi again and find a smaller outlaw ship with a small crew to borrow for a trip to Estreldez to meet back up with Bryce and Chester. Those fuckers better still be alive. For all I knew, they had made it to Estredlez and were having the time of their lives being chosen as mating prospects for the locals, like my own dreams. Well, perhaps only Bryce was having the time of his life. Chester was the patient type to hold out for what he really wanted, which was to join the tribes of Necias Prime.

We'll make it there, you big lug, I thought with a smile, thinking about reuniting with my team, finishing our mission, and living our lives.

Not that I really knew what I was going to do with mine after this was all over.

The krelin thought I was smiling at him and was grinning stupidly back at me. It took everything I had not to scowl. So what if he was helping me recover from this fume fever? I didn't trust him. Then again, he didn't say I couldn't leave the planet, and had even gone so far as to say he was planning on how to leave. Maybe he wasn't so bad after all.

"Drink," he offered a small jug. I eyed it warily, and he lifted it to my lips as his arm propped my head up.

It was that strange honey liquid that burned down my throat like it had when I was in and out of consciousness from the fever. I couldn't tell if my mind was playing tricks on me or what was real from what I remembered, but I knew my mom couldn't have been there.

"What is that?" I smacked my lips with my nose wrinkled in distaste. It was much too sweet, and yet it was similar to a honey mead with a lingering tangy aftertaste.

"Nectar," he replied simply. "It will keep you hydrated and give you needed nutrients. There are very few water reserves on planet that are consumable without being fermented through the process of creating nectar."

"So, it's a liquor then?"

"No, but there are nectar bars that serve the kind that numb the mind and body. You should rest," he suggested as he slowly pushed to stand. A strained expression on his face as his nostrils flared from what appeared to be pain startled me. My eyes widened, and anger bubbled up to the surface that I hadn't even noticed he was injured. He was tending to me, but he was hurt.

"Sit down," I barked. I wasn't mad at him. I was angry with myself.

I struggled to sit myself up right, and he again helped, wincing as he reached to steady me against the wall.

"Stop. Just stop. Where are you hurt?"

Wings spread out behind him, slowly, before he rotated to show a large clump of the same material covering my chest like a silicone adhesive, was plastered to the mid to lower back of his right side.

"I've already been treated," he assured. "I would gladly be stabbed again to keep you safe."

Had he been injured while stealing me from the Kokova?

He leaned in close and sniffed me, and I couldn't help but try to back away, only to be reminded that I was already up against the wall of the room.

"You can call me Li-aq," he said while his throat clucked like an insect talking. I tried to keep my composure, not offending him since he seemed to have been injured because of me and had been trying to help me recover. Keeping my face neutral was difficult because my stomach felt nauseous after drinking that nectar.

"Thank you, Li-aq," I said stiffly.

"Get some rest." His breath trailed down my neck, and my skin prickled with a chill that made me freeze in place.

Then he left the room, and an invisible weight lifted from my shoulders. I wasn't sure why, but now that he was gone, my muscles relaxed, and my heart hammered with an urgency that told me to get the fuck out of there.

I stared up at the light on the wall that illuminated the room in a dim glow and forced myself to move. My body ached, but at least I was alive. The stool Li-aq had used wasn't attached to the ground like the bed, allowing me to move it under where the light was. I took the bowl full of strange leech bugs and dumped the contents on the ground and then smashed the bowl against the light's casing. Instead of shattered glass or busted wiring for me to find, I was splattered with liquid. Those strange leech-like bugs filled what was once the light source and turned from clear to pink as they wiggled on the floor and stuck to my skin.

"Fuck, fuck," I swore repeatedly as I stumbled off the stool and proceeded to feel bug guts squish beneath my bare toes. Disgusted, I carefully plucked each bug from my skin and then from where I could feel the extra weight in my hair. I was sure a few were still hiding out in my damp mess of black curls, so I flung my head forward and shook it while smacking the heavy curls around. I didn't even want to think about what I looked like right now.

I took a deep breath and calmed myself to try again. The bowl didn't break, and I picked it up to use the pointed tip as a digging tool. It was probably used as a funnel to direct liquid out of the bowl, but I positioned it at the seam of where the light used to be, no longer glowing, and backlit by the only other light in the room. The casing in the wall popped out, and to my dismay there was no wiring at all.

Where the fuck were we to not have any connection to a computer and no wiring to control the filtration system of this place, no wiring to manage the lighting or functionality of wherever this was? None. Nothing. Was this some kind of backwoods tribal community on planet?

I sat there on the floor in the middle of my mess, dumbfounded on what to do next with my implant completely useless besides my translation functions. I needed to access some kind of electronics here to find Indi. Did my comms work?

Tapping my implant, I risked even my translation chip being fried to see if anything else was still working. Obviously, Indi was shut down, but maybe without the interference of the metal toxicity, other functions could be accessed?

Only silence greeted me, and my contacts didn't activate to search available connections in the area.

Then I heard a groan, and I panicked. I rushed to the strange membrane door Li-aq had left through and pushed my hands through the overlapping slit. It retracted into the walls like it was alive. With no time to focus on that, I chose a direction and moved, only for the grunt to sound again like it was right behind me, breathing in my ear.

"Where do I go?" I mumbled to myself.

"Back to me," he said, and I pivoted around ready to attack like a cornered cat.

There was no one there.

"Who's there?" I shouted down the hall.

He ignored my question and instead moaned out an unintelligible apology. "I'll find you; I promise."

My heart was beating so fast, I could hear it pounding in my ears. It sounded like he was right next to me, and yet he was going to "find me"? My brain was catching up with what was happening, and I smiled. Was my communication chip working?

"I'm going to kill him," he added with a growl.

Not sensing anyone actually near me in the hall, I continued walking before whispering, "Kill whom?"

"Li-aq."

Distracted by hearing the krelin's name that had been taking care of me, I took another step on a surface that wasn't as solid as the rest of the hall and froze as it sank down with my weight. My hands swooped out to balance as the ground flexed beneath me. I might not be a survivalist, but I knew enough to know pushing off to either go back or forward would probably tear the membrane, and I could only hope that there was solid ground beneath, but I wasn't betting on it.

"Well, fuck," I said in resignation as I decided my best bet was to spread my body out and fall backwards towards the solid surface that didn't flex with my weight.

"What's going on?" he asked with urgency.

Other than hallucinating that my communication was working? I thought with dark humor. "Just trying to avoid falling through a hole, that's all."

It would hurt landing on hard ground behind me, but that was better than falling through whatever this was. So I trust fell backwards, and my heels tore through the membrane, like I knew they would with the slightest of movements. Instinct took over, and my hands stretched behind me to break the fall, but that fucked up my plan. My hands bounced off the hard surface behind me, and my feet shoved through the membrane as I slid through. I might have made it if I hadn't broken my fall, but I had, and there was no changing it now.

So I tried to grab hold of the membrane as I slipped, but more of it tore away in my grip, and I screamed.

My elbow slammed into the wall, scraping on the way down, and I clawed for a way to stop my descent, only to hate myself for tearing my fingernails and my skin. With each swipe of my hand, I felt it even more acutely as blood dripped down my arms, and my flailing snapped something where I couldn't even ask my arm to move again.

The imaginary voice returned, echoing in my head. "Tell me where you are!"

How could I answer him in this situation? How the fuck should I know? The only response I had was to continue screaming until a buzzing filled my ears and something hard knocked the breath from my lungs.

Disorientated, I rolled and stared up from where I had fallen. Even though it felt like I had fallen for miles, it was only a few stories up from the torn membrane, and I had broken my fall by scraping against the walls. The vertical hallway looked haggard after my intervention with membrane chunks, torn and billowing in the soft air current like spiderwebs, and there was even a smear of my blood along the way.

No wonder Indi hadn't found me yet if this place was disconnected from normal networks, being illuminated by indigenous glowing leeches with detoxifying properties, and surrounded by biomaterial that filtered the air naturally.

After rolling into the nearest horizontal hallway, I screamed as my weight moved my dislocated shoulder, which had popped out somewhere along the ride. It wasn't just my flailing that helped my fall, but also several thick membranes that I had fallen through until one that was more solid than the rest held my weight.

"My arm..." I couldn't feel my fingers, and I heaved, unmoving in the middle of a hallway who the fuck knew where.

"Can you move?" His voice returned. "What do you see?"

My head slumped to the side to stare down the hall, and a head popped out from one of the rooms. She quickly glanced over her shoulder and then back at me, before sneaking out of her room towards me.

"She's coming," I mumbled before she hovered with concern in her golden eyes, and she fucking spit in my face.

I was about to curse at her when my whole world spun, and I slurred, "You fff-uuuu... ingggah bbb..." as the walls closed in around me and I felt my body being dragged across the rock beneath me.

Chapter Six
Gaven

"She's alive," I repeated over and over in my mind, but this time it left my lips and Gho-ran continued to chew on a grass reed before spitting into a bowl to create more krelin thread to attach to my broken loh.

He licked his lips before gulping down from a jug of nectar and then replied, "I have the whole mountain being searched, as well as warriors being sent to local smaller hives in the area. We'll find her and Li-aq, but we need you to stay alive too."

Gho-ran poured the contents of the bowl into a cylinder, and then pushed down a crank on the side that sliced a thin layer of the solid krelin thread that hung from the bottom like peeled skin. He squeezed one of the gua worms and rubbed it between his fingers to keep the krelin thread from sticking to him and placed it on my forearm, delicately adhering it over my loh. The krelin thread was so durable and breathable that it protected while also allowing my loh to absorb radiation; we used it for injuries on Estreldez as well. When our loh healed, it simply melted off. It was good for our planets to have peace for multiple reasons; trade agreements were only one of them.

But, if I couldn't find Li-aq and make sure the fallen queen was neutralized, then it was possible our fragile peace would shatter. That was what my mind should have been focused on, but the only thing I could think about was finding Ashley.

"I hear her," I confessed.

"I haven't heard from Queen Mab in a few risings." He mistook my meaning. Krelins were a hive mind species and could hear in their heads their queen or other krelins that they'd developed a strong bond with... like a mate.

"No, the huemoon. Sometimes, I hear her. She is, or was, with Li-aq. He is alive, but she doesn't always hear me, like the link in our implants is malfunctioning, and I heard her scream. She's injured but alive. She has to be alive."

I clutched at my gut, because part of me believed I'd know if she had died. It wasn't even a thought that had occurred until after I had said it; it was unusual to have link access to a female that had only just arrived on top of the fact that I had crossed a line with someone else's mate while under the impression I was dead. Guilt tore through me, and I couldn't even bring myself to look Gho-ran in the eye.

"I'd like to say that her screams would have made it easier for my warriors to find her, but our hive is well insulated, and the layers of hewve lard and hive structure make every sector of the hive soundproof. Only a krelin close by would notice her movements, but not her sound, through their kan," he replied dismissively, and anger boiled at his obvious lack of concern.

My hand shot out to grip his throat instinctively, and he did not move to avoid it, nor did he retreat. How could he be so calm about a female brought here to be his mate and an insurgent sure to cause destruction in the hive being nowhere to be found. It was improbable. How could he not see that?

That didn't even include the irrational thoughts flooding my mind about his unworthiness to claim Ashley as his mate if this was how he acted towards her wellbeing.

"Why do you suppose it's unlikely your warriors will not find her through her screams or neutralize the threat to your hive?" I asked carefully with strained resolve that this was his chance to prove to me he could not simply be trusted to be a friend but trusted to help me do what needed to be done.

Gho-ran's answer would be the difference between us working together or me walking out that door without him and taking her back to Estreldez where she was originally routed to arrive, regardless of being unable to claim her myself.

His jaw tightened, and a muscle twitched under his eye before he replied, "Because someone has betrayed me."

"And what are you going to do about it?" I prodded further.

"What have I done about it?" he corrected. "I don't just earn the respect of the hive by being appointed by the prince or even by Queen Mab. They left me here to deal with this mess because they believed in me, but our planet needs more than one strong hive and disorganized chaos around it. We need another hive, one that will grow in peace, not in competition."

Krelis would benefit from a more cohesive hive than the binary main hive and the outcasts scattered with smaller hives across the planet. Gho-ran would need to travel the planet and gather the outcasts or set up a place for them and make it known that they were welcome. None of that was possible while the main hive was in danger, but if he were to protect this hive, and then start his own, the news would spread, and he'd have the respect of his hive.

"What have you done?" I prompted him to continue but removed my hold of his throat. He had already told me what I needed to know, that he wasn't blind to what was happening under his watch.

"The only place to hide in this mountain that my warriors don't have complete access to are the Kokova suites. Domsal is in charge of searching the suites discreetly, but this method takes time. I have my own contacts in the Kokova that will find my mate and Li-aq. They will wait for contact with Domsal to protect themselves if they do find her."

Fingers dug into the meat of my palms as he spoke of his mate. The top of my gums ached as if I were to claim her as my own. I'd already dishonored myself and my clan by believing I was worthy of being sired, let alone claiming a mate. My heart thrummed in my chest, reminding me of what I'd already done.

Estrelds weren't carnivores; we ate minerals and rocks, but we did have mating fangs released when we claimed a mate or had offspring requiring us to drain blood from animals for their diet before their own teeth grew in. I grew fangs for Bina when my mating loh first emerged, but it was not my place to seek another mate. The huemoon deserved a mate that could provide for her, and that wasn't me. I forced myself to unclench my fist. If I hadn't dreamed what we'd done... then I had already done the unthinkable.

I groaned with frustration and held my head in my hands, both to hide my shame and to remind myself that the pressure inside of me was real.

Find her.

Find her.

My mate.

It was like every fiber of my being could not exist sitting here doing nothing while she was out there and in pain... without me. I had felt what it was to have her. Though I knew I had forever changed, I could not ask the same from her. The way she smelled, tasted, and consumed my essence would be with me always like an ethereal dream. I would find her, but I knew I could not have her when I did. Gho-ran didn't know she had left the mountain; that much was clear. He was a smart first commander of the hive, and he was unassuming with his jovial and seemingly flippant attitude. It was odd yet reassuring to see him take things seriously.

"Gaven," he reclaimed my attention. "I need a queen for there to be another hive."

Of course he did, I thought bitterly, as my chest heaved with an unsettling reaction to knowing he was referring to Ashley.

He continued, "I saw the way you reacted to the female when I brought you here."

Did he know what I'd done? How I had claimed her as if she were mine to have? I bit my tongue and kept my face neutral. I would not make him feel bad for being the better male for her. Gho-ran could provide her with what she wanted... offspring and a life of comforts that I did not have to give.

"If I am to share a mate with any male," he said firmly, "I'm glad it will be with one I call klohvin." His words caught me off guard, and I stared at him, on the verge of denial before I settled with giving him the respect of the place he'd earned over the cycles since I'd intervened on that ship to help him.

"I cannot claim her." The words sat heavy in the air as I said them, and an ache grew within my chest. Hadn't I already done just that?

Gho-ran gave a slight nod in understanding and then sighed. "I don't know if I can do the same either. Being a first mate to a hive queen isn't part of my plans, but I'll serve when called to the task. I will find my mother even if it means destroying the whole of Nala Mountain."

There was a deadly look to his eyes as he stared not at me, but past me. The ghost of his past haunted him, and any worry I had that he was going to give his all to finding Ashley and Li-aq vanished. He believed me about his mother surviving what should have been a killing blow by his brother, and he was there for me when I had been left for dead by Li-aq's warriors.

"I trust my warriors, Gaven," he said with venom. His throat clucked as his kind tended to do when their emotions were riled up. "If I was betrayed, then the only explanation is that she's here and she's regained enough strength to take control through the hive bond. Their mind is not their own, and I've set a trap to find out who is undermining my efforts. The only one I can trust is you. Will you help me, Klohvin?"

An insurgency within an insurgency. We were spies among the spies, and finding the one under the queen's control was our best bet in finding the queen and ending the divide between the krelins, but the only one I wanted to find was the one that haunted my own mind.

"You think the queen knows where," I stopped myself from saying "my mate" and forced out the words, "the huemoon is?"

Gho-ran grinned like a fool, and his wings expanded as if readying for battle. "I think she's the one that stole her to begin with."

"Li-aq?" I was putting the pieces together and stared at Gho-ran in shock that I hadn't thought of it myself.

"I've known Li-crap since we were spawn; he's annoying and an all-around stiff lard, but the only crime he's committed in his life was being loyal and ambitious. He'd happily follow Queen Mab or my brother if they promised him a fertile mate bond and a commanding position in the hive.

"He's only in trouble because he won't come forward and prove he was being manipulated, either because he still is being controlled or he's too proud to admit his mind was not strong enough."

"And if he was doing this on his own, following the queen's orders without being controlled?"

"Then the whole hive would eat him," Gho-ran said dismissively. The image of such an act was far more disturbing than simply executing him. Estrelds didn't eat flesh; we only added blood that we gathered into our meals without harming the beasts that provided it.

If Li-aq truly was being controlled by the queen, then I could thank the goddess I hadn't succeeded in killing him. Thinking back on what he had spoken of when we fought, was it strange that he hadn't wanted to kill me?

"If the queen has the female, what does she want with her?" I processed this information out loud.

"The same thing she's always wanted," Gho-ran insisted with a fire in his eyes, "To fulfill the prophecy and save the hive.

As mad as she is, she's always wanted the hive's success at any cost, and she doesn't trust anyone to do it but herself. If it means culling her own warriors, her own spawn, or crippling our females, she'll do anything to follow the markings within the Kai Mountain Oasis."

"What do they say?" Knowing her motives would help us catch her.

"A great molt fever took the seven great hives by storm, and only two queens survived: Queen Kai and Queen Leahme. The carvings were from before the great fever that spoke of two queens that would bring about the rise of the great new hives born of two species. The new krelins will save our planet and grow to rule this sector of the universe to protect it from an ancient being called the World Destroyer."

I filled in the blanks and reasoned what that prophecy of ancient text might have meant to the fallen queen. "As the only surviving queen, she takes full responsibility for saving the krelin species, but she must not believe it is being saved by merging our species?"

"There's more," Gho-ran insisted; "it is said that the great hives of the seven mountains will rise when a queen's spawn burns through death and the black star births the cure."

"So, she is looking for the spawn that survives death..." I trailed off before I could finish the thought that the black star was the one stolen from this very room.

And the spawn that survived death was sitting across from me. This wasn't a prophecy but a curse. I'd lost her before I'd ever had a chance. The feel of her soft skin nuzzling my nose was but a dream, and if the queen thought she was the one coming from the great hives... I could only hope that was enough to keep her safe until we found her.

Chapter Seven
Ashley

Waking to a killer headache, I grumbled and turned with a hiss. The fall returned to me, remembering the deafening popping sound when my arm had come out of socket. Thankfully, I could feel my fingers. Someone must have reset my arm.

"You're awake." A woman spoke in Krel, the tongue of the krelins. I debated whether I should acknowledge that I understood her or pretend I only understood Trillix or my own language, English. Sometimes you gained more information if they thought you didn't understand them.

She continued, "Most of us don't have translators, so for both of our sakes, I hope yours isn't damaged."

All I knew how to speak was English, so if she didn't have a translator, how would she understand me? This would be interesting. "Where am I?" I grumbled while prying my eyes open. She stood near the membrane door and kept her forehead to the wall, her back to me. She was tall and had an intricately laced leather-like top with long layered strips that appeared like wings dangling from her shoulders, but they were nothing like the wings I had seen on the other krelin warriors, and these certainly weren't anything but ornamental clothing to represent wings.

"Rveth is saying many tongue. Yours Egglish. That good. Teached for Gho-ran when wishing mates," she said.

"You mated with Gho-ran and taught English to him?" I tried to decipher.

She shook her head. "Learned him to teach behbe. Keep piece of old."

I understood her better when she spoke Krel because the translation was easier than hearing her broken English. If she had gone through all the effort to learn a language to teach her kids their heritage of being a hybrid human-krelin, then I guessed telling her my translator wasn't broken would be okay.

"You can speak Krel. I understand."

"Thank Lenkal," she breathed out in relief. "I understand better than I speak, and I was hoping to practice more as our spawn learned from him. I have mated with Gho-ran many times, and he has yet to produce a kantos to carry our eggs. He is

65

infertile, and I've been keeping the blood of our unborn family to feed our kantos when he's finally found a mate that makes him fertile." She sighed and slowed down to say, "I tell you this, because if you are his mate, I wish for your blessing to have your spawn carry the life of their hivemates."

I wasn't sure I was understanding correctly but wondered if she was asking me to drink the blood of her miscarriages to feed a future child made by a krelin named Gho-ran and myself?

"Fuck no," I sputtered, but then her wide golden eyes stared at me with a bit of a sheen forming around the edges. I realized she was being very vulnerable with me, and she had technically saved my life by pulling me out of the hallway. With effort, I tried to rephrase through my shock. "I mean, if I was Gho-ran's mate, then I would think about it, but I'm not, and that's a conversation you can have with his mate."

I hope she understood what I was saying, because if she didn't have a translator to get the nuances of English, she was going off of whatever she had been taught.

"You are not the black star," she mumbled thoughtfully like she was trying to process what she should do if I wasn't Gho-ran's mate, like she thought I was.

"I don't even know who Gho-ran is." I remembered the name being used when I was burning through the fever, but that was when I thought my dead mom was trying to shove soap down my throat. I couldn't be sure of what I had heard or seen.

Bright green eyes stared at me in my mind, and warm, smooth skin wrapped around me as our noses ran along each other before I almost kissed him. That couldn't have been Gho-ran, could it? My heart hammered in my chest with embarrassment at how my body was reacting to that green-skinned statue of chiseled perfection. He wasn't a krelin...

I shook my head. It couldn't have been Gho-ran. Could it?

The name had been used, and he was the only male I saw in my fever.

No. Yes? Maybe?

My body tingled all over, and I shivered to shake the feeling away.

"Please do not tell Gho-ran about my eggs; it will make him sad, and he has other worries," she confided further.

"I have no reason to say anything," I assured her. I didn't even know her name.

She nodded and pulled a crown with two small black horns on it from her black hair. "Hold still," she said while she placed the adornment in my mess of black curls. "These were the kan of Panala, a queen of Krelis."

My hands shot up to stop her, but she kept the small horns, no bigger than the tip of a pinky finger, firmly on my head. "I couldn't possibly—"

She cut me off, "These were given to me by Domsal for safe-keeping until Gho-ran was ready to give them to his mate."

"I'm not," I insisted.

"You need these to claim that you are his mate and stop Queen Kai from using you to harm him."

"I don't understand..."

"Whether you are or are not the black star, doesn't matter. It matters that Queen Kai believes you are, and if you claim Gho-ran as your first mate, then you can sway the believers to follow Gho-ran instead of Li-aq. Whoever is the black star's mate will lead the hive towards the end of the World Destroyer."

My breath caught on her use of the term World Destroyer. Was it a coincidence that that was whom I was hunting? I wasn't superstitious, but my mother sure had been, and now, I couldn't help but hear her words haunting me from the grave, "You'll walk amongst the ashes. I never understood why your father wanted to curse you with such a name. Hardships will follow you wherever you go."

"Ash trees are healthy for the environment," I mumbled under my breath. It meant dweller of the ash tree meadows, not walker among ashes, but there was no convincing her I wasn't some kind of death omen walking the Earth with a magnet of chaos at my heels.

I was hunting the World Destroyer, and there was some prophecy on a planet I was rerouted to that spoke of a black star's mate and what? Was Gho-ran the black star, or was I, in this scenario?

What signs did they have that said I was anything?

"Why can't you be the black star, or whatever?" I insisted.

"News of you has already spread through the hive. You are the flightless worm whose very blood ran black and burned through the fever."

"I can't stay on this planet," I insisted. "I have to get back to Estreldez."

At the very least I had to find a way to contact Indi and make sure my team was okay. I'd had some kind of connection with someone for a minute in the halls, but he'd been silent since I had awoken. My implant must have been completely fried, or I was losing my mind.

"Where is your closest computer?" I pivoted the conversation, hoping if I couldn't convince her that I wasn't some black star, at least I could find my way out on my own.

"The hive keeps things as our ancestors have done before us. If you need advanced resources, we have the war fleet yard where the ships dock for repairs that can't be accomplished in the orbit station. You won't find anything in the hive."

"Where is the shipyard?"

"On the desert rock beyond the Hewve Dunes. She confirmed it wasn't anywhere close to where we were. I was getting frustrated; there had to be some kind of technology in this mountain.

"Then how do you communicate with anyone?"

"Through our kan." She pointed to black nodes that lined her cheek bones and then pointed to her temples. "Queens form larger kan like our males."

Like the ones that I was wearing, I thought, but they were so small. I mean the only difference in size between the ones on the headband I was wearing and the ones on her face were that hers were more like moles, and the ones on the headband protruded like studs. They probably disappeared inside my curls, so I wasn't sure anyone would notice I was wearing them at all.

"This allows us to sense nearby movements in the hive, and we can sense when we need to gather, hide, fight, or flee. Only a queen can hear what we say and relay that information to another krelin. And mates or bonded warriors can speak with each other without words. Gho-ran's kan is strong. He can tell when someone is lying to him." She grinned fondly as she explained, "He always won ThewKapa," which I assumed was a game specific to Krelis that involved detecting lies to succeed.

As thankful as I was that she had made sure the other krelin couldn't find me and for resetting my arm, I didn't have time to waste getting out of this mountain and making my way to the shipyard.

My hands were covered in a strange layer of wax that was so thin it worked with my movements and was almost see-through. I had done a number on my hands while falling. Road rash, or in this case, cave rash,marred my legs and arms.

I was sore but recovering so I suspected a medpack had been used. This whole escape was unraveling into a cluster, and without Indi to help me hack into a non-existent system and find my way out, I was in trouble.

"He sounds... useful?" I awkwardly tried to compliment her obsession with this guy named Gho-ran and then tried to get back to the real issues. "Are there any outlaws in this mountain?" There was no way that every advanced technology had been confiscated. Someone had a connection, regardless of being in a mountain, right?

"There are a few we should avoid being seen by, as they are known smugglers—"

"Perfect." I tried to speed things along. "Where are they?"

"Gho-ran has the whole mountain looking for you," she said with bewilderment at why I would use the word perfect. She was probably writing it off as a language barrier issue.

It would be easier to take over a smuggling ship if Chester was with me, but I wasn't helpless.

"What do we know about the World Destroyer?"

She sucked in her lower lip in contemplation about what she should say and then sighed in resignation. "I was hoping the black star would reveal more about the danger foretold by the ancients."

Another deadend. Got my hopes up for nothing, and the krelin could see my defeat and quickly added, "Domsal used to serve the main hive, and she would know more. We should stay here until she comes. I could take you, but it's safer for her to come to us."

"When is she supposed to be here?" I wasn't going to wait around forever. What did she do here, anyway? She didn't stay in her room all day, did she?

Her throat echoed a clicking sound, and she shook her head, confirming she didn't have an answer for that. "She was just here not long ago... it could have been a few risings. I don't have much time before others wonder where I am, and that would attract more than Domsal's concern. My blood type is popular among our hive," she said with a smirk.

I lifted a confused brow. What I wouldn't give to have Indi translate some local customs or Bryce to do research on alien intelligence? He may have been annoying when calling me the boss and acting like an idiot, but I trusted him. Being on my own was a stark reminder of how much I relied on my team to focus on other things while Indi and I paved the way of hacking through alien technology.

Out of everyone on the team, I was replaceable. Indi didn't need me to help the team; he could finish the mission without me. That was both comforting and depressing.

"Your blood type?"

"I have a rare blood type that many warriors at the hive hatchery who want to make sure they have a kantos come for me to preserve their future before joining the war fleets."

I still stared at her, and she pulled at her shirt awkwardly. "I've helped many warriors activate their kantos resin. The kantos hold fertilized eggs and preserve them until they grow. With a universal blood type like mine, they can create a kantos regardless of whom they wish to make them for. Many female warriors bring their chosen mate to me if they can't activate the resin themselves.

"When Queen Mab returns, we will hold a Tos Celebration to have her bless the growth of our kantos offerings."

"So to whom do you offer your blood: the males or females?"

"Both," she said with pride. "With the coming war, I have a full schedule, as do all the other universal blood types in the hive."

She was moving towards the door, and I quickly questioned, "Are you leaving?"

Not without telling me more about where I was, I thought with a sudden nervousness about being left alone. That was a new feeling to me. A flash of green eyes made me grip the bedding I sat on. Why was I thinking of my dream again?

I'll find you, he had promised.

I scoffed and pushed away from the bed. What was I thinking? Some alien from my dreams was going to rescue me? This wasn't some fairytale.

Chapter Eight

Li-aq

Once again, I found myself standing before the nectar caves uncertain of why I had come.

"I'm beginning to think you have a crush on me," Xokol teased, and I clicked at him with annoyance. My kan ached from the vibration, and I restrained myself from reaching up to touch them. It was considered a weakness to reveal how much they hurt recently.

"The only thing crushed will be your own skull if you insist on trying to mate with me," I clipped back. Though I did not hold any humor in my voice, he laughed it off and offered me a gorn of nectar that was stamped with a seal indicating it was medicinal and would relieve my pain. He was perceptive for a nectar harvester.

"You should consider seeing the healers instead of patching yourself up with a nectar boost. I've been talking with Nalverc, and he wanted me to ask you if you've been having trouble remembering things."

My wings shot out in warning, and I pushed past my pain to lower my horns at him to show I was not afraid of skewering him for talking about me. "You know they could kill me for being here!"

He didn't seem alarmed or intimidated by my fierce horns or my impressive wingspan. Xokol sat down to stare at the rows of fermenting nectar and spoke as if I had not threatened him at all. "I didn't give your name, but he seemed concerned that, if you were having memory problems from the pain, it's possible that you're in early stages of molt fever. If you don't get help, you could be a danger to the hive; plus molt fever makes you vulnerable to being influenced by powerful kan control."

"I'm not weak," I snapped.

"I didn't say you were, but there are warriors with strong affinities, and your kan are large, you've been sensitive to other's abilities since you were a spawn, and Gho-ran forced you to admit you had a crush on him and wanted to be his klohvin."

"I was not forced into any--"

He cut me off, and in my embarrassment at my spawn days, I allowed it, "You've been a right lard thrower to him ever since. I'm not blaming you, but if you do have molt fever... I don't want to see you miss a chance to fight it and prove to the hive that you are not to blame for their troubles."

"You think I care if they believe I'm a monster?" Oddly enough, I turned to see what his reaction would be and answered that question myself.

"Don't you?" Xokol shrugged, not expecting me to answer, and for that I should have been thankful, but who was he to tell me what I was? "The hive is active with rumors of prophecy said to pull us from the worry of extinction. It's said that a mate of the black star will lead us to the recovery of seven great hives and time of prosperity where we are keepers of not just our planet but the entire sector of this universe."

"Why do I care about this prophecy?" He was sure to tell me what else I should care about.

"Because I thought of you when I first heard of the rumors. The hive calls Prince Trent the Black Death, but that is because he's used his poison."

I rubbed at my sore arms where my ki stingers rested. No one was supposed to know.

"He isn't the only one who was spawned with the blessing of the royals, and Queen Kia wasn't the only one who was known for such a gift."

My nails lengthened, and with the use of my kan to sense his location, I could easily snap my hand to the back of his braided hair and grip it back until he arched with a shocked gasp. I leaned over him with measured and quick precision to breathe down his neck.

"You know nothing," I warned with my throat clicking naturally to help my kan locate my surroundings. No one else was here to witness our interaction.

Still smug as ever, Xokol smiled and rasped, "My spawnmaker was an elder; he taught me of all the great hives. You know this. Stop denying who you are. Many of us will follow the spawn of Queen Sarak."

"There is no proof," I snapped. All I had was the sign of the black poison in my veins, and I was still haunted by the quick and gruesome death that had come to the hewve that had frightened me as a spawn. I was too weak to ever allow my veins to go dark again.

For much of my growth, I respected and followed Prince Trent because I believed he was my brother... I believed I was the rumored missing spawn of Queen Kai. What a fucking idiot... Blindly, I had followed Queen Kai, wishing for her favor, her acknowledgement of who I was, her son... a prince of the hive.

"I'm no prince," I finally admitted to myself.

That much had been clear when Gho-ran had come forward as the missing spawn, verified by Domsal, who had personally taken the spawn from the hive spawning caves.

I was nothing. I released his hair sharply with a shove and went back to brooding over my lost memories. If Xokol was correct about the Molt Fever, then it was probably his hope that

I was some lost spawn of another queen... it would be the only hope I had to survive how far along my fever was.

Remembering how I even came to be in the nectar reserves was nothing but darkness. All I could recall was a strange voice I didn't recognize floating through my mind, "Stop," it said with a tremor.

A sudden strength came through me at the sound, and I heard my queen's velvet caress that filled me with warmth. "Take her. She is yours; I've given her to you. Just as I promised you. Take what is yours, my son."

I shivered, and I knew I had forced myself to leave the room with the sweet sound of a female's gratefulness, "Thank you, Li-aq."

Leave, I repeated to myself.

"Get some rest," I said with exhaustion, the smell of a fresh claiming filling my nostrils. Had I claimed her without properly courting her? I shook my head at the memory. She'd had the smell of having drunk my blood, but there was something else mixed with her scent of ebbing arousal... another male.

"Fuck," I used the word I'd heard Gho-ran use often in his distress, and it seemed fitting as I threw the half empty gorn of medicinal nectar against the cave wall. It had shattered with the force of my throw, a feat not easily accomplished that I wrote off as having hit a sharp edge of rock. My aim was true, I assured myself.

Xokol was wise enough not to say a word but sit there in silence with me as I collected my thoughts. There was something safe about the walls of the nectar caverns, a place where my kan weren't overwhelmed with sensations, and even my implant, normally discouraged in the hive, was disconnected from the universe. The interference of an implant with how our kan worked wasn't an issue for me. If anything, I hoped the implant would deafen the pain of how often my kan connected with... everything.

Chapter Nine
Ashley

I had hesitated to leave the room as swiftly as I had before. The hive was a dangerous place to wander without knowing when the ground would be firm or nothing more than a membrane I could fall through. Being found again and tended to should I almost die was improbable. Whatever luck I had in this universe was sure to dry up soon.

First, I had been recovered from the person who purchased my contract. No longer under the control of a slut shack was a bonus, but then I had easily escaped from the person who recovered me only to then fall to my almost death and be taken in by another kind krelin.

I wouldn't try my luck for a third save.

But, I couldn't just stay in here either.

With a deep breath, I pulled myself together to exit the room. A static buzz made me shiver, and I heard a noise that I was sure I imagined.

"Operation Wizard. Message Repeat. Operation..." It was Indi! I pumped my arm, only to suck in a sharp, painful groan at the pull of my still injured shoulder. The message only repeated once more before going silent. He would probably keep on repeating the message in intervals just to let me know that he'd located me at least here... but how?

That would mean there was some kind of technology in this mountain. Indi's message was broken and weak, but somehow, he had been able to put a small message through technology with the ability to connect with my implant...

"I hear you Indi," I whispered. "We're going to make magic happen and get the fuck out of here."

I winced as a pain shot through the back of my head, and I held my ear as I doubled over.

"You left her in your room?" The voice was more clear than Indi's had been, the voice from my dreams.

"Of course not," said the krelin that had just left me not that long ago, her voice almost a whisper compared to the one before it. "She's in one of the unrenovated rooms that are abandoned for personal use by Domsal herself. It's in the hive section Gho-ran and a few other spawn grew up in when the Kokova was first rebuilt one room at a time."

"And you left her there?" He repeated what was obviously his point to begin with.

"I couldn't bring her through the hive; someone would notice her."

"Was that where you found her?" His voice was demanding, and it sent a shiver through my body in a delicious way that I knew I didn't have time for.

Those words repeated in my mind, I will find you.

How was I hearing this?

"It's likely who Gho-ran is looking for is on one of the upper suites. She took a nasty—"

"Quiet," he interrupted her, and everything went silent as my breathing hitched. "Ashley?"

I gasped. He knew my name? Of course he did; this was obviously some kind of delusion to think the alien from my sex dream was actually searching for me.

A low growl softly came through, and I felt my thighs squeeze in reaction before he spoke again. "Can you feel me, Goddess?"

Something about the way he called me goddess made me shiver with anticipation of what we'd done the last time he called me that. Was that not a dream?

"Am I dreaming?"

It was possible I was still fevered and passed out in the room, right?

"If you can hear me, it's dangerous for you if someone finds you before I do. The fallen queen of this hive isn't dead, and she could be in anyone's mind, at any time. She believes you are some prophecy that she wants to control. Stay hidden until I arrive."

If he wasn't a dream and I had fucked an alien in my fevered delirium, then surely his cock was the reason for the ache between my legs, but that didn't mean I could trust him. A good fuck didn't mean he was any better than the rest of the aliens here.

I touched my head, almost forgetting that I was still wearing the headband with the tiny horns on them. These seemed like they had been important to someone, so I attempted to take them off and return them to the room I'd left.

Static electricity zapped my fingers as I touched them, and I winced as I heard his voice crackle through my implant, "St-whe-ooo-rrr."

Then there was silence as I held the headband in my hands. What the fuck? Curiosity got the best of me, like it normally did, and I put the headband back on for a beat to return to the back of my neck, and his voice returned, but he wasn't speaking to me, "Take me to where she is, now."

"You'll bring attention to—" she gasped, interrupting her own words which were barely more than a whisper in my ears, "Skybender," she shockingly called him.

"Lead the way," he demanded. His voice sounded like he was under water, and I removed the headband again.

I stared at the tiny horns in wonder. Somehow, these krelin horns helped my implant tune into the frequency of the alien from my dreams. Was this how they communicated with each other? The hive mind?

Metal toxicity hung in the air of the planet... Horns connected with technology. Were they related? The message from Indi? Was the whole planet a natural transmitter? Fascinating, I thought with awe.

Bryce would be obsessed with this planet if he was here with me now. Chester would probably be asking them to make him his own set of warrior garb, I thought with a smirk at what I was wearing. The top was a combination of some form of leather shoulder guards that layered in flaps down my arms and a strange molding resin that held my chest in place and traveled up my neck with that same pinkish coloring of one of those larva bugs. It was a pretty color and complimented my dark skin tone, but I didn't want to think about how they got that coloring... was I covered in bug guts and who knew what else to create the clothing I wore?

I could already hear them making fun of me for being disturbed, considering Earth wasn't much better. Bryce would say something like, "The headwrap I normally wore to sleep was made of moth worm secretions after they were boiled alive." It wasn't the first time he had defended Chester with his blood fascination within his necia warrior obsession.

I would be lying if I said I didn't find some of the things they spoke of about different species to be intriguing. My hand lifted to my neck, and I remembered the way heat seared through my skin when teeth grazed with tender kisses. His green skin had glowed as he moved a top and inside me, and my fingers had dug into his flexing back muscles. I bit my lip at the thought of doing that again.

My back to the room, I hesitated returning the headband if it indeed helped me communicate with whatever transmitters were on this planet. Clutching the adornment to my chest, I couldn't trust that anyone was going to let me leave this planet with a whole prophecy being formed around me. Did I think I was some prophecy fulfilled? Fuck no. They were desperate and needed hope to cling to. They'd quickly find someone else that matched their broad stroke prophecy when I was gone.

Keeping my steps close to the walls, carefully I made my way through the hive tunnels. One thing I had noticed when I fell through the last membrane was that next to the wall there was a lip of rock that was around a foot wide that could be used to walk across. Even if I came across another drop in the hive, I was betting they were all created similarly.

What are you doing? I thought to myself as I got farther from the room. An ache built up in my gut at not waiting for the big green glowing alien to find me.

"I have a job to do," I reminded myself.

Find access to Indi, regroup with Chester and Bryce, and then follow the trail to Al-Hez.

The cave was becoming more and more rough looking, as the membrane and plaster used for most of the hive I'd seen was becoming less and less until even the domed lighting filled with glow bugs turned into actual cave walls with veins of sticky sap dripping down with pinkish bugs crawling in the muck. It smelled like metallic blood in the air as I walked on with more certainty that I wouldn't be falling through these floors.

I scooped up some of the bugs and reluctantly squished them in my palm and rubbed them on my skin like a salve. They were supposed to help make sure I didn't get metal toxicity again. I'd rather be covered in bug guts than die from the metal I could taste in the air. My elbow lifted up to cover my nose and mouth with the leather flap on my arm.

It had been hours since leaving the room, and with my free hand, I removed the horn adornment from my waist band and put it on to test my theory about the metal in the air and the krelin horns acting like a lightning rod for transmissions.

I winced as it seemed to zap me like static behind my ears.

"...repeated. Operation Wizard. Team on site. Message repeated. Operation..."

Team on site... What did Indi mean? Had he found Chester and Bryce? Were they on Krelis?

The message was garbled, and not as clear as when I had heard the one called Skybender.

A draft made me glance up and see a tunnel up above with signs of more krelin membrane to return to a more maintained section of the hive. The layers of leather overlapping on my arms caught on an updraft, opening like tiny parachutes. The breeze tickled my bare back, and I noticed there were leather flaps at my shoulders that hung down the back and lifted, catching me on the wind slightly. I leaned forward only for my face to be blasted with a stronger gust that whipped my hair around into my eyes. Turning from it, the flaps at my back caught the wind burst, and my feet left the ground as I squealed.

The onset of focused air through the cave tunnels eased, and I floated back to the ground with the leather on my legs and arms and off my shoulders acting like an air balloon with the hot air. The wind burst again, and this time I embraced it, diving farther into the stream, and I lifted up even higher with another excited yelp that turned into laughter. How were there not more krelins around here to enjoy this natural wonder? They must have, considering their clothing was made to utilize it.

The metallic taste in the air dissipated as I ascended. The gust of warm wind ebbed and flowed until I reached a ledge I could grab, and I swung myself through to the membrane lined tunnel. Something sweet and tangy reached my nose.

As I turned a corner, I heard the rush of water before I saw the golden liquid waterfalls churning a small wading pool. I quickly pressed myself against the wall to be as small as possible, rocks biting into my back through a thin membrane, to avoid the attention of several krelins gathered in the area.

They must not have heard my giggles on the way up here because of the sound of the liquid sloshing against rock and creating a natural echo in the cave. My chest heaved with nervous energy, and I inched along the wall slowly towards the other opening I saw around the waterfall.

Mist pebbled on my cheeks, and I licked my lips, realizing that the moisture tasted like the nectar that had been given to me before, and I was so thirsty. I didn't believe in animal instincts that perhaps my body was searching for something to feed my energy to keep going, but I did believe in luck.

And I was surely running low on any of that if I had somehow found an entire pond of nectar to drink but had to keep going.

Mumbles of noises came from where the krelins talked, hardly heard over the waterfall, but somehow my translator picked up what they were saying because the clicks of their throat echoed, and they weren't whispering to keep their conversation private.

"Another one?" she asked with incredulity.

"Four hoomans, and one of them placed his strange fingers to his throat and called to Gho-ran when he went to defend the hive from the ship that got past our warships. Do you think the bigger ones are females or the smaller ones?"

"Does it matter? All we can do is play with them if they can't make a kantos for spawn." The other female krelin laughed awkwardly.

"They are so smooth looking," she said with intrigue. "I wish to rub myself against their downy layer; the one that mate called has a tuft of fur on their chin."

That didn't sound like Bryce or Chester; they were both pretty diligent with their grooming, but it was possible it could be either of them if they had come straight here. Indi didn't specify what team was coming for me, and part of me knew I was replaceable. They both should have moved on without me.

"You should not encourage mating with a species that has no kan or wings," the other warned.

"You said all we could do was play with them..." she pouted.

"What if you got attached and wished to steal another warrior's kantos from the reserve? You could end up getting the hooman killed in Rakin. You said they didn't have any claws or fangs."

"I liked his mating call," she said with a huff. "It was a nice sound."

"You should stay away from them; you were there to help defend the hive, not to mate with them. You are a warrior with unmatched blood. We must protect the Blood Blessed and prevent extinction."

"None of them suffered from the Fume Fever," she remarked, and I could be thankful for that. They were safe, even if they weren't Bryce or Chester. That was good news.

I was sure they had been sent by Indi, whoever they were.

"What will Gho-ran do with them?"

"I didn't have the chance to ask; that's actually why I brought it up..."

"What is it?" she grew irritated and another male krelin approached them.

"If you are not donating to the nectar, you should leave," he warned. "This is not a place of gossip."

"Xokol," the female smiled with her fangs on display, "we are not the only ones who use this place for talking privately."

"Your words are hardly private," he countered. I would agree with him, if I hadn't been annoyed that he interrupted crucial information about what had happened with Gho-ran and her thoughts on what might happen to humans on Krelis or even potential clues about where they were now.

"I did not wish to worry the hive unnecessarily without asking advice from a High Kloro warrior," she reasoned.

The other krelin clicked her throat and demanded answers, "Now!"

"Gho-ran dismissed protocols and took one of the hoomans, flying off with a smaller one in his arms."

Even the one called Xokol leaned in and pushed for more. "What else did you notice? Did he musk the area?" When the female was flustered with the questions, he slowed down and added, "Think, Enbir, what do you remember, and who else was there to witness?"

"He–He– I don't know?"

"How can you not know if he used his musk?" the other female snapped.

"Well, the other hoomans didn't faint or seem affected in any way when he left."

"What direction?" Xokol asked.

"Away from the hive..." she mumbled softly.

"Goddess Lenkal have mercy on us that he returns before we face King Sylve's forces." The female paced around the pool of nectar.

"What should we do? The hoomans were very upset, and the bigger one claimed Rakin in vengeance. Everyone will know about it soon. The hooman said something about returning the one called Faith, unharmed, by next rising or they will have their A.I. send out the data about our planet that it was gathering to our enemies."

"Why didn't you lead with this information?" The krelin female clucked with irritation.

"This would not have happened if our Queen was here..." Enbir said with distress. "She should not have joined the war fleets so soon."

"I miss the certainty of feeling more of the hive when the queen is near," the other female krelin agreed.

"You think we need the queen more than the ships that pro-tect us out there from the threat?" Xokol reprimanded both of them. "What we need is more than one queen, and if Gho-ran took the hooman, then the goddess has blessed us with the chance to have a new queen."

"What are you saying?" she asked with uncertainty, clearly eager for the answer.

"Gho-ran comes from royal blood, queen's blood, not just in blessing but from her own dropped eggs, using the kantos of strong warriors. His spawn will be powerful. Mated... his kan will grow more powerful. We will have seven great hives again, as prophecy says we will."

"But we have no other queens' blood... It would only be two great hives."

"The black star will lead the way to the hive's future," he stated without explanation when something jerked me behind the waterfall, and I gasped before a hand covered my mouth to muffle the sound.

Fuck.

Chapter Ten

Gaven

My skin burned for her, sensing she was recently where the krelin said she would be, but wasn't. I was supposed to meet back with Gho-ran hours ago, but I couldn't let the coil around my heart unwind.

"Mine," I growled before leaving the female krelin wondering whether I had indeed followed her or simply disappeared.

With the heat of my loh radiating in waves, I knew that Ashley had gone in this direction. Tracking her went without thought. The gua worm residue yet to be absorbed into the membrane along the walls where she was likely to have pressed her back while carefully moving through the passage was only a confirmation of what I could already feel. And with Gho-ran's help, I was able to better navigate the hive by keeping an eye out for ledges in the ceiling. They were used as a way for those without wings to climb. If there were ridges in the walls that was a sign to jump over the gap or grab hold of the ledge and move past. I could easily see as my radiation got close to the handholds on the wall that gua residue from small hands had crossed over with no signs of torn membranes or her trail ending.

Gua was only a temporary solution to knowing I wasn't losing my mind. Its glowing property would fade as it was absorbed, and I was sure to help speed up that process as it came in contact with my loh's radiation. I knew I was getting closer, moving faster, and my heart raced at what exactly I would do when I found her.

She obviously didn't want to be found if she left not only her captivity from Li-aq, but also the safety of the female krelin's care. It was likely she trusted no one, and I would have to convince her to stay with me.

For a brief moment I thought I could hear her subtle breaths in my ear as she said, "I've got a job to do. Focus. This isn't a dead-end; this is going to be the way out. Just a long way out... Fucking naturalist aliens and their lack of technology. A map would have been fucking great," she grumbled before the line went silent again.

I chuckled and agreed a map would have been preferred, but to the hive the map was already in their minds. Krelins could easily navigate the tunnels with their kan.

Krelins didn't keep technology in their hives; their warships and docking yard were plenty for them. They preferred having their information be for the hive only, and what better way to ensure that than to keep all their history with elders and tombs guarded deep in their hives?

The smell of blood was growing stronger, and the heat in my chest ebbed as I approached a heated air pressure shaft in the hive. I couldn't sense where she was any longer as the bursts of hot air blew through the space. There were no more signs of the gua residue, a few hours of moving through these passages having passed. I couldn't have been that far behind her, not with how quickly I moved to catch up.

Gho-ran would know by now that I was not joining him to meet up after he investigated the incoming disturbance near the mountain's deserts. We each had our own priorities, and an understanding between us solidified after he had given me a nod of approval and said, "Go find her. If any of my warriors have news, they are informed to meet at the bathing cavern."

I stayed hidden, waiting for anyone to approach the empty gorn and do something to indicate they were using it to send a message. Gho-ran told me that other gorns would stack there when emptied, but one gorn always stayed, never refilled or taken back to the nectar pools.

I'd gone. I'd waited. I'd "found" her, but here I was at a dead end.

Standing at each cross path to this steam tunnel, I tried to sense where she had gone with the same certainty I felt when following her here. My chest remained cold at each intersection, and that feeling like I could find her anywhere quickly dissipated.

Was I imagining things?

Was this all some fevered delusion?

Was I searching for any sign and imposing my own will on even the residue of gua larva that could have simply been from someone tending to the lights? I refused to think this tug within my chest was nothing.

The pitched squeal of the pressure building in the large hole at the center of this room told me the steam would release again soon. It was then that I glanced up instead of thinking about the possibility of her having fallen to the depths. I was reminded of the oversight that had me close to death when matched with Li-aq.

I hadn't expected he would wait for me on the ceiling and ignored the very fact that many warriors had wings, because on a ship, where most of my missions were, none of them used their wings often. Traces of membrane could be seen above, and I shook my head.

How would a huemoon with no wings make it up there? Had she climbed?

The pressure released from the opening, and I put my arm out and felt the force whip my arm up and push it out of the vortex. She was so small, I thought with amusement. I glanced up again. My loh molded out, forming hooked blades along my forearms.

Up it was, I thought with determination as I dug my loh into the wall above my head and pulled up to dig my other into another hold. One after another, I anchored myself and lifted myself up the tunnel.

After noticing how hard I had to cling to the wall with even my legs anchored in when the pressured steam came up again, I decided to utilize the lift and detached myself to launch up faster before digging into the wall once more before the airflow faltered in strength.

It was then the heat in my chest tugged once more, and I knew I had made the right choice. She was close.

An excitement coursed through my veins as my blood pumped faster, and I pushed off the wall and into the new tunnel that was more maintained than the area below. Gathering my loh's radiation, I focused it to heat up and cycle to hide myself from krelins' perception. The smell of blood intensified as I moved forward, but it was much too strong for it to be the blood of a single life form.

Voices of krelin clucked through the echoed chamber, but their tongue was too difficult to understand when multiple sounds were vibrating against the walls and their voices were too soft to catch the pauses from one voice to the other to make out words without activating my translator. I tapped behind my ear and hoped they wouldn't notice the vibration of their own voices in the translator with the echo of the room.

"What are you saying?"

A few krelin were speaking, and I inched closer to the waterfall, both to mask the sound of my movement and also to add to the illusion my heat produced to hide me from their eyes. A tug was pulling within my gut and aching deeply the closer I got, and it was then that I saw her. She was not well hidden; if the krelins decided to truly look, she would be spotted when their distraction faded.

"...Mated... his kan will grow more powerful."

They were engrossed in their conversation, but it was difficult for me to hear their words as my own focus was captured by how the shadows played across the form of the beautiful female. Moisture clung to her full black curls, and her skin was dewy from the waterfall churning the blood-filled pool below.

Inching closer, I could see the concentration in her dark eyes, and I overheard them speaking of how the black star would lead them to the hive's future, and my shoulders tensed to stand taller and... protect her from the harm that could come from a whole hive believing her to be some kind of prophet. I'd learned my lesson from believing without question of a leader's guidance. My own Almder had disappointed me in her betrayal that I had no desire to return to Estreldez once Mabel was safe.

Mabel... I hadn't thought of her until this moment as I stared at... a name resonated in my mind, but I could not bring myself to say what this huemoon meant to me. My heart hammered, and skin tingled with heat deep down to my bones, vibrating in my loh.

The conversation between the krelins ended, and the silence beyond the crash of the waterfall was deafening. It wasn't something I'd tried before to put someone else within the heat waves that protected me from most prying eyes. Working alone was easier, but perhaps if I grabbed her and put myself in front to block their view, that would be enough with the added distortion of the waterfall.

The clicking of their throats resumed, and I knew they would pass by us soon. I wrapped my arm around her waist and pulled her with me farther behind the waterfall. My other hand was sure to cover her mouth as it opened in shock, and then I pressed myself against her curves.

My breathing heavy on the top of her hair as I cradled her, I found my cheek rubbing against her strands enjoying the way every caress of her against my skin filled me with a strange comfort. Her lashes tickled against my forearm as her ass shifted against my thighs. If I wasn't towering over her, I thought about if I'd bent my knees more and shifted my position, those little movements would ride higher where my mating loh could feel her.

Then I felt her shift the opposite direction, and her elbow landed squarely on my mating loh with a hard jolt.

"Fuck," she grumbled under her breath, and I prayed that the krelins wouldn't notice as they left the nectar reserves.

I was lucky it wasn't my cock she had impacted with such force, but there was a tenderness to my mating loh when I was on the cusp of arousal that had it softer than I would have preferred. Waiting until I couldn't sense any stray noises from company, I finally addressed her.

"Are you okay?" I asked first, wondering if her elbow had been harmed by the impact.

"How are *you* okay?" she questioned back while holding her arm protectively.

Acting quickly, I hadn't thought about whether she would see me as a threat instead of shielding her from view.

She continued when I wasn't sure what to say in response. "Do you aliens not have a dick?"

That confirmed she had indeed been aiming for my cock, and had circumstances been different, she would have been successful. Instead of being upset, I was pleased, thinking that she had possibly given Li-aq the same kind of reception.

"Unless you were planning on mating with me, it remains sheathed behind my loh, which can be harder than most stones."

Did she remember that we had already mated?

"Like a cock pocket?"

That was hardly the most pressing issue we were faced with, but I would humor her. "Estreld cocks are formless until they harden to shape to our mate's preferences. Even after forming for a mate, it is sheathed when not in use."

"So a cock pocket," she reiterated, and I was pretty sure I heard her chuckle.

"Is this humorous?" From the interactions I'd watched of other huemoons who'd joined the mating ceremony, laughter could indicate being uncomfortable. With the krelins gone from the room, the only thing stopping me from moving away was my reluctance to build distance between us. I enjoyed the way her temple rested on my forearm, even if she was simply avoiding scraping her delicate skin on the rockface. She was still rubbing at her elbow as her hips settled back against my thighs. The movement made it difficult not to think about how she had straddled me within her, and her release had squeezed my cock into submission. Moments like this one made it difficult not to believe that had all been my imagination.

"No more than anything else in the universe. I couldn't tell you why there are slugs with cocks as large as their bodies, which seems cumbersome to have a majority of their guts actually be space to hold their dick. I imagine it all coiled up like intestines, and the image in my mind was like fucked-up spaghetti." She chuckled again, and I wasn't sure if that was a good thing to relate my cock to, but the need to defend myself made me believe that it was not an endearing image to be related to spaw-get-tea. Even if there was an upward trajectory of "fucking," which by the way Gho-ran used the word was usually referring to mating, this spaw-get-tea seemed to be similar to guts, which were not sexually appealing.

In a moment of unbridled agitation at the correlation, I carefully removed my arm from cradling her head and took a step back. The air, though warm here because of the heated draft close by and the humidity of the waterfall, was cold with the lack of her skin on mine. She turned around, and I could see her eyes dilate to take in who had startled her. I watched as her pink tongue slipped over her lips and was reminded once more of how she tasted. The slit of my mating loh warmed and softened with the hopes of releasing my cock, and a stubbornness came over me.

I was patient. I took precautions when choosing who to sire myself to, and in one swift dream all of that changed. I shouldn't have her, not when she wished for a family and joined the exchange for mating with someone capable of giving her that safely. The warmth building in my chest grew, and my loh ached for her touch. She was my mate, even if I wasn't hers. I'd committed a grave sin in claiming her, but what was done was done.

"Goddess," I called for her attention, and her eyes finally blinked. "When you think of my cock, the only image in your mind should be of me, and me alone."

I watched as her hand reached behind her to grab onto the wall. Her breath was coming out quicker now, as her chest rose and fell with those pretty lips parted in invitation. She was not laughing now, and my leathers were thankfully an estreld design that Gho-ran retrieved from the main hive's trade stocks. They were made in layered flaps that protected while also allowing the user to remove sections based on individual loh placement, and as our loh were much stronger than leathers or stone, we usually kept them exposed... including our mating loh.

To many visiting species the mating loh simply appeared to them as ornamental plating matching our loh. Most of the clan wore light garments that hardly concealed anything, but the mating loh were a slightly darker coloring to the rest of our loh. Males who had activated the formation of their cocks within usually displayed them proudly. It was an honor to have fertility, and on the off chance that our cocks triggered the dropping of a female's eggs, they were a sign that they were actively searching for a mate.

My hand reached out for hers, and there was no objection as her slender fingers slid against my palm. Guiding her touch back to my skin, I told her, "It was not a dream as my cock filled you, and these fingers dug into my back."

I traced the outline of the top of each of her fingers as they stayed above where my heart pounded with nerves. Would she reject me? It would be wise for her to use that elbow of hers or even her knee to hit me in my mating loh once more. It was tender now, the slit forming to allow my cock release. Her blow would sink into my loh and find its intended mark. I feared that it would be more than my cock that would feel such a sting.

The way her muscles tensed, and her thighs rubbed together for stimulation told me she felt something for me. It was less obvious for huemoon females than with estrelds. When an estreld female wished for pleasure, it was known by the way she glowed and the mating nerve below her slit pulsed. It didn't mean she was fertile or that her eggs were dropped in preparation for mating, but it was an invitation to give her pleasure in hopes that she would trigger such things.

For huemoons, I'm told they do not have the same fertility process as our species. They had cycles of fertility so frequent that the Almder sent Loric to Rworth, their planet, to negotiate contracts for our mating ceremonies to be ongoing. I got nervous about the way my cock pushed against my mating loh to be released. I had already done something unforgivable by bonding with her as if I were sired to her and without her permission claiming her as my mate.

For me, mating could never be for offspring, no matter how much I would love to have one. My thoughts boiled in sick darkness before the hand I had not been holding to my chest touched my cheek. Cupping my face, she looked up at me with a furrowed brow between her beautiful brown eyes that were nearly as black as tarnpul. It was as if she saw the torment within me, and she pitied me. Instinct made me pull away from her touch, and an ache grew deep in my chest.

But her next words made the guilt of claiming her even greater, because I was unworthy of such a female and she deserved better.

"You're right," she said with breathless words, "This isn't a dream. And even if it were, we have every fucking right to enjoy whatever pleasure we can get out of this fucked-up world."

Chapter Eleven
Ashley

His skin was so hot, even my sweat evaporated as soon as it glistened at the back of my neck. I thought my scalp would be itchy, but the thought quickly left my mind as he traced my fingers, caressing them gently like they were each precious jewels.

I enjoyed the way his touch tingled down my legs and into my toes. He was the one I thought I had imagined. His touch. His voice. His heat. I'd known as much when he spoke, but it wasn't until I saw him that I truly accepted that he wasn't a dream, that he wasn't someone I wanted to run away from, but instead towards. I didn't know why, but I didn't care to know at that moment.

He had kept his promise to find me, and now I'd finally know if he was part of my team or just another obstacle between me and my mission. But before I could tease him and demand he tell me if he was going to drag me away somewhere for my safety, he pulled away. It was both a relief and agitating. He wasn't going to force me anywhere, but he was fucking backing away from me.

I should have yanked him back and demanded answers, but the look in his eyes stopped me cold. What was that feeling that stirred this uneasy desire to comfort him? My mind and body were at odds with wanting to shake him or fuck him, while another part of me wanted to stroke his short, pale green hair to soothe him. He still held my hand to his chest. I could feel the strong pulse of his heart and that slight ease of tension just before he was going to release my hand. That was not how this was going to play out, I thought with determination. He reminded me of a wounded puppy that had been told too many times that it didn't deserve to be touched, to be fed, or to live.

A kindredness within me recognized that look in his eyes as resignation that this wasn't something he was allowed to have. That was my fucking decision, not his. If we wanted this, then who was here to stop us? The krelins were already gone, and I had seen how he had materialized out of nowhere to shield me. He was fully capable of hiding us by some strange alien camouflage should we need it. My hand lifted to his cheek, and I made sure he was paying attention as I reassured him, "You're right. This isn't a dream. And even if it were, we have every fucking right to enjoy it."

I didn't care if I was going crazy, or if he was simply a side effect of my mind coping with the madness of being trapped in a mountain and barely surviving an alien fever from metal toxicity.

"A better male would return you to the huemoons or even back to the contract you originally made with my planet."

Stopping him before he could continue, I remarked, "I don't want a better male." I wanted the one standing in front of me to do something about the ache between my legs.

This wasn't some marriage proposal. I didn't have any hangups about the attraction that was undeniable between us. We'd already done this before, but with the fevered heat, I had enjoyed it, but there was this disconnect between reality and my mind. Not this time, this would be all mine. He would be all mine, not some patched together bliss that I could barely hang on to, but mine, a memory that I could hold on to as something that wasn't just a dream. If it happened twice, how could I still claim it was just something my mind made up?

"Prove to me you're real," I said while slipping my hand from cupping his cheek to behind his neck. I gripped the shorts of his soft green hair to tug him down to meet my lips.

Static zipped through the contact between us and heated deep within my stomach, radiating down to my core. His hand pulled mine from his chest and tugged it behind him to wrap around his waist as he gripped the back of my head and slammed us back into the wall. His hand cushioned me from the impact, and his other arm was on my lower back snaking its way around my hips and under my ass. Our kiss deepened as he growled, and it sent shivers of anticipation through me.

Yes, I thought with a thrill as I felt his fingers massage between my legs. The krelin outfit I wore was mostly well-placed strips of leather and layered plating that wrapped around my legs more like crotchless chaps. They had helped catch the air in the heated vent of the cave to float up here, but there was nothing covering my wet cunt from those probing digits once the strange flexible resin melted away with his heated touch. How my own skin didn't dry out from the heat pulsing from him, I didn't know and didn't care. It felt good, and that's all that mattered.

His grip adjusted, as I basically was sitting on his forearm with one leg clinging to his hips, my other on tiptoes. My own hips rotated, and his fingers slipped away to hold my ass. I whimpered my objection at stopping, but a new sensation filled me as something firm rubbed against my clit that hadn't been there before. I could feel where both his hands were, one cradling my head, as I bit on his lower lip to pull a moan from him, the other holding me up as my legs wrapped around him. I wasn't a small woman, and my thighs were bigger than his forearms, but not once did I feel him tremble from fatigue. All those tremors through his muscles were because of my cunt as it rubbed against him like he could feel pleasure from touching the outside of his pants. I had yet to see his cock, but he'd confirmed that it was stored inside of him, and if I hadn't imagined things before, he indeed had a cock.

Reluctantly, I released our kiss to glance down between us where our bodies met, the folds of the krelin wardrobe draped around us on either side. I shivered as my hips rubbed along him, and that's when I saw the dark green jewel glistening with my juices split at the center, revealing the firm head of his cock. That jewel wasn't part of his pant's protective plating at all; it was all him. Holding tightly around his neck with one arm, I used my other hand to slip between us and guide the large head of his cock where I needed him. It notched at my entrance, and I groaned as his cock pushed inside me, edging as I moved the tip in and out.

Biting my lip hard, I could feel his cock growing deeper inside of me as I ground my pussy against him. My head pushed back as I held back a whimper. Sliding on and off his cock, it was longer each time I moved until I stilled at the sensation of something like a finger slipping between my lips and pulsing at my clit. He groaned as his fingers dug into my ass, and his forehead dipped down to bury in the side of my neck.

He whispered into my ear, "I'm not a good male, Goddess, but I will have you even if I must ruin you for all others."

Oh stars, it was like he knew exactly how to talk to me to make my insides shiver. His hips thrust forward so deep my arms clung tightly around him, and I shouted, uncaring of who heard me, "There! Right there, Fuuuck," I whimpered towards the end. There was no fear about being discovered, because I knew that if someone were to interrupt us, he wouldn't live to tell the tale. A sick part of me liked the safety of knowing he would risk his life, and I had full faith that it was no risk for him at all. Did I want someone to die because I craved feeling the fullness of ecstasy as he plowed into me so hard my breasts bounced with just enough force to stimulate my nipples against his chest? Of course not, but my pussy spasmed around his thick cock just thinking about him going feral for me.

I wasn't a good woman. I'd been betrayed too many times, and I refused to live with regrets and unkept promises.

Right now, in this moment, I could fuck this alien god like there wouldn't be a tomorrow and use his perfectly carved cock to feel things I hadn't felt in ages with no remorse. Would he still be around tomorrow? My chest ached as I thought about living this dream just this once only for us to go our separate ways. Why was I so frustrated from a future event that hadn't even taken place yet? I didn't know. But I rage fucked him for it anyway, as I worked my hips against him and moaned as his dick hit at an exquisite angle deep inside of me.

His words sent me over the edge as he grunted with each grind of my pussy against his second cock at the base of him slipping against my clit. "You take me so well, Goddess."

My pussy clenched and spasmed as my forehead pressed into his. Our hot ragged breaths mingled together until my screams came out as nothing more than air and his lips returned to mine to consume every noise I made. The ache moved from my chest down between my thighs, more than enough to know it was real, that this moment was real as heat flooded through me to the tips of my toes, down the back of my neck and shuddered deep in my core.

As the waves crashed through me, I slumped against him at last in stunned silence. What the fuck was that? I wasn't some angel without a past, but the passion, the primal way he took everything I gave, was nothing short of a huge mistake... This wasn't supposed to be addictive. This was supposed to be accepting that there was something between us and then moving on. But I didn't want to move on. And that was the problem, wasn't it?

We were surrounded in a gentle green glow from his jeweled skin, and I didn't even realize when he had moved me to the floor, still buried within my pulsing greedy cunt. I stared up into those green eyes, both of us panting as our chests heaved.

I was already ruined, I thought as I stared up at him from exhausted and heavy lids.

And I didn't even know his name.

Chapter Twelve
Gaven

Black curls clung to her forehead like they were molded to her dark skin, and I found myself fascinated by even the smallest details about my mate. I wished to stare at her for many moons to map out every curve, dip, and crevasse, like the wonderful fullness of her lips as I sucked the lower one into my mouth, grazing it with my fangs. I wished to hear her Earthling words echo from her mouth again but didn't want to risk that another krelin would come back and interrupt what I had planned for her when...

Then it hit me square in my heart as I watched the way her eyes fluttered with exhaustion.

When what?

When I took her back to my home on Estreldez? When I would be denied the right to keep her as my mate the very moment she stepped a precious foot on my planet's soil?

My Almder would not give her blessing, and I had no other home to give this amazing female that somehow called to my very bones. My life was one of modest means. I hadn't even prepared a proper dwelling to impress Mabel with when I had intended to offer being sired to her because there was no need, not when she preferred living at the palace with Princess Luan and I was away on missions off planet much of the moon's rotations.

I had lost everything worth giving to a mate long ago when Bina rejoined the great rock. She was named after our farthest moon, the moon known for representing adventure and the possibilities of the beyond because of the way it pulled and struggled to stay in orbit around Estreldez. Just like her name's sake, she was never meant to stay but to explore the great beyond.

The goddess below me startled me from my thoughts as I traced one of her curls along her hairline and behind her ear. She cleared her throat and glanced away shyly, and she was anything but such a sight, though I admitted it was endearing to see the flush of her cheeks. I knew better after the way she rode me so fiercely to think she was above telling me what was on her mind.

Finally, she spoke as my lips quirked up, enjoying the sight of her squirming about something she wished to say to me when she had been so vocal before, "You know... for someone who promised to ruin me, I didn't think you'd meant you'd be giving me a complex about whether you had enjoyed yourself." Her voice grew stronger and stronger with each word, and then she ended with an agitated huff.

I blinked at her in confusion. "You were," I corrected myself immediately, not really used to having someone take my cock and then not running away immediately after, "are everything I could ask for."

"Then why?" she snapped with a groan, then turned her face away from me once more, chewing on her lower lip. This was obviously difficult for her to discuss with me, and annoyance rushed through me at the implications of what was happening.

It was not unusual for a female on my planet to wish to mate with me because my cock was formed from having already had a mate, and they often came prepared with an ointment provided by our medical lab technicians to reduce swelling so they would not be forced to lie with me until my knot released us.

After a time, I simply expected it and had the ointment on hand myself so I would not feel offended and agitated when they struggled to reach their clothing to pry themselves away after they'd been satisfied.

A sudden and visceral uneasiness overcame me that she was feeling this same way now, eager to part with me, and I had no ointment to withdraw myself.

"Why," she repeated, but my mind was buzzing and this hollowness made her voice sound distant to my ears with the realization that I did not wish for her to feel the same way as the others. "Then why do you look so fucking sad with your cock buried hilt deep inside of me? I'm not a charity case!"

"Charity?" We didn't have an exact word match on Estreldez for it, but my translator said something about the act of giving gifts. She was a gift from the goddess, but I didn't believe that was the answer she was looking for, so I abstained from saying anything on that matter and diverted to assuring her she was not who made me sad; it was the exact opposite.

I thrust my hips into her and ground myself in her warmth to get her attention, eliciting a moan I knew she was trying not to indulge in.

"This cock isn't mine," I said, while moving just enough to make my second cock work against her mating nerves that tore a beautiful curse from her pretty lips. "It ceased to be mine the moment you took it."

Her fingers dug into my forearms, and I thrust again, working my knot deeper. I could feel the tip of my nerves striking a firm barrier at her center that made her shudder each time I made contact.

"You fucking bastard," she hissed as she gripped me tighter, and the heels of her feet dug into my ass. I felt the strangest thing happen as her walls flexed around my cock. My knot pulsed and

116

eased its hold, allowing me more movement to pull back and slip inside of her once more.

This had never happened to me before.

Her head flung backwards, and I held her in place by her hips to speed up my timing and increase my power as my second cock rubbed between her slick mating folds and my main cock pounded within her. The noises she made of encouragement were sending me over the edge I hadn't known I could cross again. It was as if her body were the stars, and I could do nothing but burn in her embrace.

As she panted and mewled below me, I felt as if I controlled the very galaxy with a thrust of my cock, and a devious grin was permanently plastered upon my face as I stared down at her in wonder. "Do I look sad to you, Goddess?"

She only replied in grunts and moans, ignoring my question as she writhed, and her nails scraped my arms. I was used to being handled roughly, though usually they were my enemies that didn't survive the consequences, and her nails were too fragile to do any real damage, merely superficial.

So, I asked her again, "Do. I. Look. Sad. Goddess?"

"I love it when you call me goddess," she rasped, again ignoring my question, and it made my grin widen. I could feel my fangs protruding, begging to taste her., to have more of her inside of me.

"Fuck," she panted, and I could feel myself giving way to my release with her walls pulsing around me.

I growled and moaned with pleasure as I stilled inside her, my cock swelling. The knot resecured for a second time.

We both heaved with a shudder of warmth, and I couldn't keep the smile from my face as I stared down at her. Even the thought of her not wanting this faded with her response to me. I was beginning to see that perhaps her words did not match up with her feelings, and that eased my worries.

But it did not stop her from asking the same question, "I won't say no to that again, but I saw what I saw. If it isn't me, then what... or who?" She said the word "who" with disdain and a sense of pride filled me that though we had only just found each other that she was jealous of a who she'd never known.

"There is no who," I assured her.

"I also said what, but you replied with saying there was no who. There is always a who," she said with a shiver as her muscles relaxed, and she frowned at the pink marks she'd made along my forearms. It was just a surface scratch that I couldn't even feel, but she rubbed at them like her fingers were erasers that would remove the marks. I would gladly wear those marks for the rest of my cycles but admitting to her about my past felt like losing her too soon.

It was inevitable that she would leave when I had nothing to offer her, and if I returned to Estreldez with her, I didn't trust the Almder to allow us to stay together, even if it meant forcing me to go on missions that would keep me away from her long enough to find her another mate.

I used to have such trust in my clan, in my leader, but after what had happened to Mabel... it was misplaced.

I sighed in resignation, since Ashley was more than worthy of my trust and deserved to know the male she'd mated with and to know the risks involved in being with me. I could not provide her with offspring, not if it meant losing her to the great rock.

With a nod, I distracted myself by taking one of her hands and tracing her fingers as I held myself up on one elbow. I smiled once more at the stretch and pull of feeling myself buried within her, my knot securing us so at least I knew she'd hear me out before running away.

"You are right," I began. "Everyone has a who. I have two." It was strange to say that and mean it. I had been so hopeful that Mabel had understood me and had mistaken our friendship for the possibility of more, and here I was not even including her in my count. It felt right not to include her as a who of the past. I cared for her, and I thought we could both use our friendship for companionship, but she wasn't the past or my future.

"Two!" Ashley groaned, and I could see I had lingered too long before explaining, and the heat in her cheeks grew. Leaning over, she quieted as my lips kissed her temple.

"Yes, two." It wasn't what many would think of. They were the only two that really mattered; everyone else was just passing the time, easing the hurt, numbing the cycles until I could return to the rock we had come from. For the first time in a long time, I wanted to tell someone about them.

Gho-ran knew, but he had found out on his own, and we didn't discuss things. He had a habit of sticking his nose into my business, but he never used the information against me, so I didn't bother bringing it up. Even Loric knew, but that was discussed with the Almder as a requirement of disclosing my curse before working closer with him on sensitive missions.

"My daughter never had a name, but many spawnlings aren't named until their Rising Ceremony when they are bathed in the moon's light and given the Almder's blessing. In my heart, I call her Nabi, her mother's name, but inverted as, instead of pulling away like the farthest moon Bina, she will be pulled into my heart until Lumei takes me."

Chapter Thirteen
Ashley

My heart pulled towards him as he spoke of a child he never got to raise. I was ashamed to admit even to myself that a lost family was not what I was expecting him to say with that cheeky smirk playing on his face. Tingles rushed down my fingers as we pressed palms and then laced and unlaced them like a game to keep feeling that rush of warmth pool within me.

I'd never felt so giddy before, and I'd certainly never stayed attached to someone long enough to truly look them in the eyes and listen to them talk about their past.

His daughter didn't survive birth, and he lost his mate all in the same day. But what he told me next had me burning for an entirely different reason that made me want to punch someone in the throat, and it might as well be him for internalizing it for who knew how long.

"You have a right to know that I cannot provide you with offspring," he said with a steely expression. I was surprised at how much that knowledge sat heavy in my gut. Having children wasn't really an option yet, but after hearing him say that, it reaffirmed that some part of me wanted that for my future.

I remained quiet as he continued, "I won't stop you from taking on a mate that can provide that for you. On Estreldez, it's not unusual to take on sired males in service of your needs, but I will not make this endeavor difficult for you as I do not wish to simply be sired to you. Other mates may be your sired, but I will be your mate, as you are mine."

Still processing this information, I felt my mouth gape open as I stared at him. Was he implying I should be finding another male to get pregnant? I mean we had fertility clinics on Earth, but it didn't sound like someone would be taking donations and implanting them. It very much sounded like he was offering for us to add another person to whatever this thing was between us.

I wanted to punch him for already thinking he wouldn't be good enough on his own. So what if I couldn't have babies with him? I hadn't even thought about what kind of life I would have after Al-Hez was found, and I could certainly introduce the concept of in vitro fertilization if kids were an issue later.

Later?

Fuck, was I already thinking about this future? This was like jumping into the deep end and finding out it was actually the ocean, not a pool at all.

"Mates?" I choked on the word with an awkward smile. "Not exactly what I imagined when you said you'd ruin me. I was thinking more of this," I motioned to where our bodies were still linked.

His eyes hooded, and a finger trailed over my nipple as he promised, "I look forward to ruining you in more ways than this, Goddess."

I loved when he called me that. "But we cannot stay here longer. I've heard movement deeper in the nectar caves; there must be another entrance other than the heated vent flow."

"Right..." I had almost forgotten that we were trapped in a krelin hive within the mountains. My walls clamped around his thick cock still warming my insides, and I wondered what exactly we were going to do with his knot still swollen. Before I could ask, he cradled me close, and I was lifted up while still attached. With my full weight seated on him, I felt him deeper, and I moaned, receiving a chuckle from my response. Did he just laugh at me?

"It is not uncommon after a mating ceremony to find couples like this long into the rising third moon." After a moment he chuckled again, and my cheeks burned. "I never got to experience it myself, and I am quite fond of it. Perhaps, we should do this often after I kill the queen."

"After you what?" I asked, a bit caught off guard from enjoying my personal dickmobile and the pleasant idea of this being a regular occurrence being casually referenced next to an assassination.

"I can't leave until I make sure the threat to this planet's survival is eliminated, and if we are to believe the rumor we overheard, then Commander Gho-ran is not up to the task if he's disappeared with one of the huemoon visitors."

My crew! Indi. He could help, and they certainly weren't going to leave without whoever was taken; if it was a woman then I didn't know who it might be.

"By the third moon, how long exactly are you going to carry me like this?" Not that I was complaining exactly; it felt like pleasant tingles floating through me as he walked, and I clung to him.

"It varies from estreld to estreld, but a mated female's loh are capable of controlling a male's cock. Bina would often just reduce my cock to a nonsolid state when we were finished, and we never participated in the mating ceremony. It would take cycles before it would reform."

I choked on my own spit. "Nonsolid state? How does that happen?" He certainly wasn't nonsolid right now.

"When a male is bonded, our cocks form for our mate. As my mate, all she had to do was dismiss me, and my cock would return to its natural state."

"Dismiss you? Like thank you for your deposit and be on your way?"

Damn, I thought, and felt myself grip around his neck tighter. Did that mean, as a human mate, I didn't have that kind of control over his cock? Was I even his mate? My mind flooded with pesky insecurities that I wasn't used to feeling.

"Could I do that?" I asked sheepishly.

"Dismiss me..." He stilled and adjusted his hold under my ass, only needing one hand to hold me up with my legs wrapped around him. His other hand laced through my knotted hair, and nails scratched along my scalp, like a massage before they gripped and tugged lightly until my chin lifted to stare into his green eyes. "Is that what you want?"

"And if I said it was?" I challenged, but my fingers tightened around my elbows to keep him locked down. I thought about how he could just slip his head out of my hold if he really wanted to, but then my ankles crossed, and my pussy clenched down on him like that would do any better.

"For any other, I'd say that is the Goddess' will, and do what I could to ensure your happiness regardless of my involvement."

"For any other," I repeated breathlessly as I watched his lips like they were a dessert I was ready to devour.

"Not for you, Ashley of Rewirth," he said, and as much as I wanted to hear the rest of what he was going to say, I interrupted.

"*Humans* call it Earth," I corrected, snarking about his pronunciation of my species, and then licked my lips.

He grinned mischievously, not offended by my loudmouth. I couldn't help myself. The filter on my mind was broken, but he didn't seem to care about that.

"Where you came from doesn't matter, Goddess," his hand on my ass squeezed, and I squeaked with shocked delight as he sharply pulled me against him. I didn't think he could get any deeper or that we could be any more connected. I was wrong.

"I will not be dismissed," he asserted. "When I was mated with Bina, it was because the Almder wished to have more offspring with the strength of my loh to harness the moons to disappear as our ancient warriors once did. I am a spy, Goddess; I was trained to be everywhere and nowhere. I was not unaware of why I was mated to a female honored with many offspring before me. She had helped many males become fertile, and she had done the same for me, only to find her death.

"Once realizing the curse of wanting more power, the Almder made sure I would never harm our clan again."

"What do you mean by 'never harm again'?" What had the Almder done to him?

"My seed will never be a risk to your health," he revealed like he was simply talking about what we were going to eat for breakfast. At that thought, my stomach growled, making it even more awkward to ask how they had ensured that his seed wouldn't be doing anyone any harm. It wasn't unheard of for men on Earth to get vasectomies, but with the decline of birth rates, the procedure had become illegal in most jurisdictions. It's also why our governments aren't opposed to sending us off to various planets because they are trying their hand at any methods of keeping the human species going, even if it means human hybrids.

But there was something viscerally heavy and disheartening to know that there was no future of what we could make together. It was an odd feeling to have when I had only just met him, and the only name I knew from him was what I heard someone else call him, Skybender.

"We are in the nectar reserves. There should be a gorn around somewhere. I've seen that humans tend to eat plants and meats over rocks, so nectar should be sufficient."

I cringed at the thought of having more of it, and he could see that. The darker mood of what had happened to him in the past was lightened by the immediate needs of my stomach. He smiled and admitted, "I do not have a taste for it either but have had to make do with what is available. I keep a stash of sotec bitters hidden at the shipyard, but I have resorted to eating hewve lard as a last resort. I must convince myself it is no different than eating a prepared meal by a guardian when I was an infant." He shuddered but held me securely to him. Whatever the hewve lard was didn't sound appetizing. "Trust me the nectar is a better option, but I do have moon moss when we reach the ship, which is a welcome change of flavor that has been used for many of the meals prepared for your species on my planet. I've overheard the humans call it vanilla cream."

That sounded like heaven compared to the meals I had had to eat to prepare for my travels in space. I hadn't had decent tasting food in a long time because of the additives used to help acclimate my stomach to non-Earthly foods. There were gorns scattered throughout the hive, and we came across one that I reluctantly had brought to my lips and drunk from. It tasted even worse than the one before; the aftertaste was sweet and tart with an unsettling metallic cotton that made me rush to drink what I needed to not feel lightheaded.

Voices echoed up ahead, and Skybender grabbed the gorn and gently placed it on the ground. A few drops of nectar dripped from my mouth as I was mid-gulp, and he licked it from my chin. I would have giggled, but we had company, and I froze up while the macho green alien god decided to keep walking easy like we weren't in the middle of a krelin nest that I'd had to escape from twice. If anything, did he slow down? He wasn't even trying to hide.

"They won't see us," he assured in a whisper. His fingers trailed along my back, sending shivers down my spine.

Did he hear my thoughts? How would they not see a huge green glowing alien with a human clinging to him like a monkey? We were kind of hard to miss...

"Don't go that way." The clucking of throats translated in my ear.

"Not again," the other said, sounding annoyed, their clicking higher pitched.

"Someone is always mating at the nectar pools," he complained.

I couldn't help but have the cheesiest grin on my face as I buried my head into Skybender's chest. That was us they were talking about, and it now made sense why no one interrupted us. Apparently, it wasn't uncommon to do that kind of thing there, and they kept their distance, not getting close enough to know we weren't krelins.

"They better not have contaminated the pool with anything other than their blood."

"So what if they did? What are we going to do about it?"

"This is why I drink at the Ki-Hive in Helmer Wood. At least there I know the nectar is pure."

"If by pure, you mean laced with Kalemer, then sure. I wouldn't touch the stuff."

"No, they have mating services there. New batches of homebrew delivered every cycle to be matched by nectar alone. If you match, then they will take your blood and offer it to the homebrewer, and you might find someone to create a kantos with.

"With war coming, the Ki-hive is just as busy as the Kokova. Many wish to leave something behind should they honor the hive in death."

"And you?"

A series of clucking noises that didn't translate before he replied, "I haven't seen a fresh kantos warm a growing spawn in ages. Do you see any new spawn around here? Why do you think I'm over here in the nectar reserves instead of out tasting the new nectar shots?"

"We have warm kantos," he objected.

We came around the bend of the hallway and into another opening. There were three krelins, though only two were chatting, now in sight, heading down a different corridor. I kept my mouth sealed shut, not wanting them to hear us and turn around.

I could see one of them nod and say, "A whole several hives' worth, but when was the last time you saw any of them hatch? We have a new queen, but she's off protecting the planet from invaders instead of protecting us from the true threat hidden at the hearts of every hive on the planet."

"She'll return and help our spawn thrive," the other said hopefully.

"For all of our sakes, your words to the Goddess's will."

The third spoke then, and I shivered at his deep voice that felt familiar. "They will all hatch in the great return of the seven hives."

Then their wings fluttered, and they disappeared as they flew up where I could not see.

After a time of him walking in stoic silence, I could feel his cock retract from me, storing back in his jeweled pocket, and yet his arm still held me up.

"You could put me down now," I said sheepishly.

"I could," he agreed but didn't act on it.

"Skybender," I tried saying his name out loud, and he flinched. Honest to stars, he had me down on the ground faster than I could say, well... Skybender.

There went all the feels for being fucked until my legs were jelly. And in fact, they were still jelly, and he had to keep his arm around me, so I didn't collapse on the ground in a puddle.

"Where did you hear that name?"

"Taking that isn't your name then?"

"It's what the krelins call me. Like the monster in the sky that appears out of the air to break them," he snapped. "Do you wish to think of me as the monster of the sky, Goddess?" His question was intense, and I felt my muscles match the weight of his words, bound up and tight.

"Aren't you?" I lifted a curious brow, testing his boundaries. Hadn't I told him I didn't want a good male? I wanted a male that would destroy anything that stood between us and happiness. Doubt crept up, souring my stomach, and I wondered if this was nothing more than the kind of fuck that you told your friends about in memory of the one that you wanted but wasn't meant to be.

He gave a curt nod. "I'm a monster, but I want to be more than that," he corrected himself and then breathed in deeply before resigning himself, not wanting to dwell on it, I supposed. I couldn't blame him; I had a past of my own. "It's best no one refers to me by that name. The hive would not look kindly on us. My given name is Gaven, like the Gaventil desert on the far side of Esterldez where the moons don't orbit. Rarely seen, but the strong train their loh to use less radiation to survive."

"You've been there," I stated, already knowing the answer by the hard look in his eyes.

"As soon as my loh hardened and they discovered I had 'disappeared' for the first time, I was sent there to train. I am alive today because of that training." There was a finality to his tone that spoke of the end of the conversation.

That's all he said, and I wasn't going to press the issue when I wasn't willing to talk about why I was even here.

He kept me on the inside, closer to the wall with him one step ahead of me. The hallway in front of us seemed to blur, and my skin was sweating with water I knew I couldn't spare.

My hand gripped the wall for support, and I heaved. "I need water. Nectar isn't enough."

"This way," he said, and we finally started to see rooms again. We entered one of the membranes, and it looked nearly identical to the one I had been in before, aside from the fact that the light source wasn't broken in this one.

Gaven stretched out his arm, and green light glowed from his jewels until it looked like glass being blown in the heat, and then a curved blade formed along his forearm. He sliced at the wall, cutting the membrane and whatever clay was behind it to remove a chunk. He grimaced before bringing the chunk up to his lips and bit a chunk off.

"What are you doing?"

"Getting you water."

"By eating the wall?" I asked incredulously.

Unlike me, he gently reached up and unscrewed the dome holding the weird glowing larva. Then he spit the crushed-up wall into the bowl of wiggling worms that used to glow golden and were now changing color to purple. With his mouth free from chewing, he explained, "Nectar is basically water with fermented nutrients. I can filter out most of it with the gua and ground up hewve lard."

I stared at him and then the wall with curiosity. "You're telling me the wall is made of hewve lard, and that's something you've eaten before?"

His lip curled in distaste. "It tastes surprisingly spicy for something so disgusting, but yes. The lard is hewve feces, and after knowing where it comes from, it disturbs me every time I see my clan enjoying it in all of their meals." He took another chunk in his mouth and chewed it, then spit it into the squirming glow bugs, called gua. He did that several times, and I went over to the wall to touch the hewve lard with curiosity. It was hard, like rock. Even trying to take a crumble off from where he had taken his own chunk wasn't happening. With a grunt I tried to pry a piece off again.

"How are you chewing this crap?"

It was harder than stone or cement.

He chuckled and bent down to open his mouth and point to his teeth. The tops were like carved diamonds. "These can crush bone; hewve lard is nothing." He smirked and took another chunk to chew and spit in the bowl.

I was about to correct him that the hewve lard was harder than human bone but decided against it. Whatever bone density his species had was a lot stronger than mine. Those strong teeth were nibbling gently at my neck and tugging at my lip not long ago, and after seeing him crush hewve lard, it was clear he could have broken me.

"Gaven..." I liked the name, even if it sounded a bit sad after learning that it referred to a lonely place on Estreldez.

He stopped what he was doing, the dome of gua worms and ground up hewve lard sitting in his hand. I sat on the bed and sighed. Was I really going to do this here? Now? I untied the headband from my waist and stared at the cute little horns attached to it. He didn't seem alarmed that I had it. It would have been hard to miss as we did other things, but he just waited for me to speak while resuming his task of creating a filter for the nectar.

"I'm not sure what's real anymore," I began, pacing myself before putting the headband through my hair, the ends of the black band hitting behind my ears, where I assumed it somehow connected with my implant. The little horns disappeared within my curls. I covered my mouth with my hands and whispered into them waiting to see if he could hear me. It was possible that he had excellent hearing in the room, but his translator wouldn't pick it up and know what I said in English. If he knew English then that was a different story, but I didn't think he did.

Would he hear me?

Was this all in my mind?

He turned to grab the gorn on the floor, his back to me, and then I heard the crackle of my implant communicator. I wasn't imagining it...

His words were clear as he replied, "That's only one side of the story, isn't it?"

My breath caught. He was the first one I had admitted it to, but I had to know if it was because the krelin horns helped enhance the reach of my communicator or if he had amazing hearing.

"What do you mean?"

"You talk to yourself when you think you're alone," he stated simply. "You didn't kill your mother. It may feel like you have, but she was dead the moment she involved herself."

"You heard me the whole time?"

"I thought you knew I would; isn't that why you said anything at all? You aren't a killer."

"You don't even know me..."

"Don't I?" He turned to me then, tearing a piece of the membrane from the wall and pulling it into a bag over the gorn. I watched as he flipped the gorn over, and the membrane held the liquid like a stretchy sack. He put the dome of worms and ground up hewve lard on top of the gorn and then poked a hole at the bottom of the sack to let it drip into the bowl.

Nothing happened for a while as it dripped until I heard the distinct sound of liquid echoing in the gorn one drop at a time. We were going to be here a while.

He spoke again once he tied the top of the membrane sack and hung it against a hook already prepared in the wall.

"Do you think she was alive when they came for you?"

"What are you trying to say?"

"You said that you wouldn't be here if your guardian hadn't turned you into your government for stealing their technology, which you used to help blow a whistle and provide humans with a means of accessing data your leaders kept from the clan."

"You got all that, did you?" I snipped back, not wanting a reminder that my mom thought I was a criminal for thinking we deserved to know what was happening and that our government wanted to rely on aliens to solve things. Here I was fucking one, and my government may have put together this task force, but I knew as well as the rest of our team knew that it was easier for them to get rid of us this way. If we succeeded, then great, and if we didn't, we were one less problem.

All we had was each other and a hope that Al-Hez could be convinced to help undo what they had started.

"That does not explain how she returned to the great rock," he prompted to get more information.

"I didn't listen to my government when they warned me that I needed to turn myself in so they could protect her."

"Were they not protecting her when they knew there was danger?"

I folded my arms over my chest, not wanting to hear what he was trying to get me to admit.

"They couldn't protect their own fucking tits, let alone an old woman set in her habits."

"Then how did you kill her?" he insisted.

"It wouldn't have mattered if they had protected her, but I could have. I could have made her disappear with their help. I could have made sure the open-source code I released was monitored. I wasn't dumb; I included a viral tag on the code and could have tracked its usage but didn't want to give the backdoor to the government and have them shut down access. People deserved to know what our leadership was planning for our future, but I was distracted with trying to find a hacker and didn't stop the attack over five years ago."

Dampness trickled down my cheeks at the memory of that day. My main servers were in her house, and when she contacted the government about her daughter being the Phoenix Ha cker... she had set a course for both of our lives that couldn't be undone.

Do you want to save your mother? The message on the open-source server I created had pinged to me a week prior.

I hadn't replied, and another message had come: *Turn yourself in, and we will protect her. Return our proprietary software and help our team protect Earth's future. We know you've been searching for the World Destroyer.*

Pretty words, nothing more, but I had ended up going to them regardless. If I had done it sooner, perhaps things would have been different.

I hadn't just been responsible for my mom's death but the deaths of hundreds of humans, because of where I had stored my servers, when terrorists against alien invasion and the exchange had made people afraid to travel the stars. My program and using Indi from my servers had resulted in them having access to destroying ships, exchange offices, and alien supporters across the globe.

Lost in thought, I remembered the fight I'd had with my mom that stopped me from going down to my servers that day and prevented me from seeing that someone had tampered with them. That was the last conversation I'd had with her, because the extremists covered their tracks and destroyed the servers after they were done.

They were the flashy type. It wasn't enough to fry the hard drives... they had blown up the house. They had wanted to make a statement.

A soft thumb rubbed across my cheek to gather my tears and then slipped the beads of lost moisture along my lower lip, pressing it into my mouth. I glanced up at the large alien god before me but couldn't see him past my tears blurring my vision.

He said nothing as he sat beside me and gathered me into his arms, allowing me to break apart.

Then I blurted, "I can't let it happen again."

His hand stroked my head and down my back, lingering on my hip, rubbing comforting circles with his thumb.

"Do you believe things would be better if you had never released the knowledge to your clan?"

I had never asked myself that question. My issue had never been with hacking into the system and stealing Indi. It had been with how it was used when I had been distracted. That was why I had made sure Indi wouldn't be taken advantage of like that again. He was free.

"If it wasn't me, then perhaps someone else. I will never know," I admitted, "but many people would still be alive if I'd done things differently." If I hadn't argued with my mom. If I hadn't run away and gone down to the servers like I had been planning to do.

"I used to say such things," he finally said after several minutes of allowing my sniffles to fade against his chest. "It wore on me to have sent so many lives back to the great rock. It was the Pride of Estreldez that told me that I was not a god and to claim the responsibility of one was not my place. I may have killed many, but had I done differently would those lives have taken the lives of others? And if I had not killed them, would another not have ended that life? To think that I alone am responsible for a life whether my hands directly ended it or not is inaccurate.

"For everything I have done in this life, I could not have accomplished it alone. Every life I took was about to be taken from this universe; that is my oath to the goddess. And for the lives you've taken part of, you provided the means but not the trigger. Someone else bears the weight of that decision; just as we bear the weight of our own.

"Even as a goddess, the ones who wished to pull the trigger would have found the means regardless of if you provided it to them."

Hearing it said out loud didn't change how I felt about my part in the whole thing, but he knew that and said it anyway, continuing to hold me. It may not have lessened the guilt, but there was a weight lifted from my shoulders in knowing that he understood, and it was like he was helping me carry that burden. I could only hope that perhaps he felt the same way about his own guilt, regardless of how much he shared about it.

Chapter Fourteen

Li-aq

The caves of the nectar reserves were the one place in the hive that I felt like myself without the pain of my kan throbbing. I could sit here for many cycles, sipping the nectar reserves and being alone with my thoughts. Xokol was the exception; he often wandered the nectar reserves, both because it was his duty to the hive, and also because he knew this was the place secrets were held. If a krelin wanted to know what was happening without being told by the queen herself, then all one had to do was wait and listen. This was the one place in the mountain where krelins couldn't feel the hive bond connecting us. We were just ourselves with no invading thoughts, no feeling of worry, and it was a welcome relief when so many of us could feel war was coming.

Xokol left me with my thoughts, but there was a faint tingle in my kan that had me following him through the rough tunnels behind the falls. Then I spotted her, the black star of prophecy moving along the wall towards the falling water I waited behind. She kept herself small and didn't bring attention to herself as the gossips spoke of Gho-ran's latest scandal of stealing some huemoon. I backed away slowly to hide in the shadows of the cave. These tunnels didn't have the same lighting as the main route through the nectar reserves. As long as I stayed quiet and kept my wings still, any noise I made would be drowned out by the water sloshing against the pool. My golden eyes were reflective in the night, so I crawled up on the ceiling. It was a failure of many species not to look up, and I was betting on even the black star having this weakness as well.

My claws easily latched into the hewve lard keeping the tunnel secure. As I reached the top, I swung to dig my other claw in with my back to the wall. It was uncomfortable for my wings to be folded and bent the way they were, but I couldn't afford for the sound of them buzzing to keep me lifted. The end of my wings, both the top and bottom, had sharp thorns that I pushed my heels into the lower ones to dig into the wall as an anchor to relieve the extra tension needed to prop myself up. The resistance was balanced across my legs and arms now as she crossed behind the water, unseen by the others.

I winced as I felt my kan throb the closer she got. She was directly below me, and as my senses took in her form... There, I thought, spotting what was tied to her thigh by a strap usually used by those without wings to hold an extra cloak to help protect them from the heat of the vent system when used to get to upper levels of the hive. We had cloaks made from estreld loh that were extremely useful for dispersing heat and radiation. Even the leather of our clothes had estreld loh crushed up and woven with resin into the threads. My eyes could see easily in the darkness behind the falls, and it was clear she had someone's kan adorned in her ties.

Whose were they?

Had she killed for them? No, they were much too small... if she stole them from a warrior, they would be much larger. Even a female's kan were larger than those, as they may only show the surface by a small margin. When pulled, kan were larger under the skin. We only adorned kan from warriors that were of importance to the hive. A queen, from a fallen mate for their spawn, or... I closed my eyes not wanting to admit that the kan strapped to this female was that of a spawnling that had not survived to have its kan form properly.

Again, whose kan were they? And why did she have them? Was she truly the prophesied black star that would lead the way for the rebirth of the seven great hives?

I could feel the heat rise in the already hot tunnels of the nectar springs. Quickly, I looked around but saw nothing. It didn't change the way my skin crawled, and my kan vibrated with irritation. I was more sensitive than other warriors, and it was why I commanded my own warfleets before the new queen's arrival. I may not see an estreld, but I knew the signs when one was near. Then I searched for where the black star had been and... she was gone. I hadn't heard her move or sensed her moving with my kan. There was no way she was gone.

He was here... and it took all of my control not to release my irritation through my throat.

Then I heard them, and a smile crept up my lips. I heard him grunt as she swore in the hooman tongue. They didn't know I was here and, though very faint and probably not heard over the waterfall, I could faintly hear a few words here and there when the heat fluctuated like waves, allowing for my kan to catch their hushed voices. Unfortunately, all I could understand was the estreld's words, as he spoke in Dendil, the tongue of his clan, that I had learned when I first became a warrior. My translator couldn't pick up on their words with the radiation interference, and the huemoon tongue wasn't something I'd learned.

My kan burned as I understood at least his side of the conversation, and I came to the quick realization that, though they were hiding, they were more concerned with speaking about mating and estreld anatomy... I had no need to hear about his cock or how she should only have a mind for his. I thought about whether I should interrupt this mating display by spraying them both with my musk, but then I thought about that dream-like state of sensing she had the scent of another male on her.

Thoughts of her being mine, and yet not, resurfaced as I forced myself to leave her. My teeth ground together as this urge to descend upon them burned within me but not for the reasons I expected. I thought of Gho-ran and how this estreld was known to be his klohvin. It was the only estreld in the hive, and I had no doubts that it was him hiding behind his bar tricks. There were very few estrelds that I knew of that had the ability to stay unseen as long as him. Some have tried, but their radiation had swelled and then burned out after short bursts. Still, I could not see them, and I knew it was Skybender. I held back a scoff at how disgusting estrelds were and their lack of respect of the hive and our customs. Gho-ran should handle his own business; it was not my problem that he had chosen unwisely for he had valued and pardoned the fireworm of his crimes against our hive.

They stayed still and unspeaking below me, and I could sense the others beyond the waterfall were on their way out, including Xokol. The heat of the estreld was slowly moving away, ebbing in intensity. I knew they were far enough into the tunnel behind me that I could descend silently among the unbridled clamor of my unaware warriors in their departure. I released my hold on the ceiling and allowed my wings to stretch as I fell, breaking my fall to the sound of a small patter of boots, insignificant compared to the other noises. I leaned against the wall, waiting to see what the estreld would do once he believed they were alone.

It took longer than I thought before he allowed his shielding to fall. I only moved when I sensed the heat on my left wing grow faint, as to make sure I was still close, but not too close to them. The clicking of a krelin's throat was normally instinctual, not something many had control enough to stop themselves from making a few noises in the course of simply breathing. But I was a private warrior who valued discretion and would often sneak up on my own warriors to teach them discipline and perhaps encourage them to try to control themselves better. The hive was a noisy lot, and our pride in our skills made us lazy in trying to hide ourselves, unlike the cowards of Estreldez. There was no need to hide ourselves, that I agreed on, but I also believed there was a time and a place for control. This was that time, I thought with vindication at my training efforts.

Each breath was slow and measured as to not allow my throat to vibrate and activate my voice flap, which other species referred to as sounding like clacking noises not unlike insects. They wouldn't dare say such a thing to our faces. We've killed for less, but I should be thanking them for developing this skill to be unheard when I wanted to be.

Then I heard the first of many noises that I could not unhear even if I wished to.

Was there no respect to use one's own clove within the hive? No longer caring about keeping myself hidden, as they were obviously too preoccupied and my peace already ruined, I flew up into a different tunnel to go around them. There would be no solitude in the tunnels today, and I didn't wish to listen to them any longer. They didn't seem to pose any threat, and I was not in the mood to crave a female that was already claimed. I knew from bits and pieces of my memories that she had at one time taken my own home-brewed nectar, and if she was still mating with another male after that, then she was not meant for me.

The buzz of the hive tingled down my kan after some time flying through the tunnels, and then a heaviness came over my eyes. I quickly landed on solid ground to steady myself, feeling nauseous.

"Are you okay?" another warrior asked as I waved them off.

"There you are," a soft and comforting voice filled my mind. "You know how I dislike being apart from you. Allow me to take your pain away."

Warmth flooded my system, and my skin tingled with a plea-surable sensation that made me groan, my throat vibrating with appreciation. It felt intoxicating, like the perfect nectar of a mate I craved for but had yet to experience.

"Yes," she cooed like I had done something to please her. I liked knowing I had pleased my queen. I knew that was who this was now, and I would do anything to keep her with me. I felt her ebbing from my mind, and I pleaded with her.

"Wait..."

The warrior who had come to assist me put my arm over his shoulder as he held me by my waist. "You are a heavy bastard. I don't think I can lift you on my wings. How about we stay here and I go fetch the healer?"

Another warrior hissed, "Are you sure we should be touching him? He has that glazed look in his eyes and sweat on his kan... What if..."

"Don't be a coward." The warrior at my side chittered his teeth, gnashing at his friend in admonishment for being frightened of what seemed to be the fear of me having Molt Fever. I vaguely recalled Xokol speaking of me needing to see the healer for this, but I didn't feel ill anymore, not with my queen soothing my pain.

"You allowed the black star to escape," she tutted with disappointment, and I felt ashamed for thinking it was right to leave the hooman when, clearly, I had been wrong. "Where is she?"

"They are mating," I huffed out.

The warrior next to me chuckled and sighed in relief, "Oh good, perhaps it isn't the Molt but a bit of musk on you when you ran into them." He called out in a series of throat clicks to the other warrior to tell him with a bit of humor, "Don't go that way. There's another musk bomb down that way."

"For goddesses' sake," the other cursed. "Don't they know that mating in these small tunnels usually knocks out anyone who passes by? Musking the nectar reserves should be punishable by hive humiliation."

"And what would you have them do? Mate for all of us to see?"

The other choked on his own spit in disgust. "No, I don't want to be caught up in someone else's mating musk. I'll end up like this guy, all loopy and confused about if I should be mating, sleeping, or fighting. Look, he's sweating, and his claws are out. He's liable to cut you up and stick his dick in you at the same time. Let him sleep it off."

"I'm not opposed to a good dickin'," the warrior who had set me inside of a resting net that he pulled from the ceiling said while making sure my wings weren't bent awkwardly. "Look how large his kan are; I bet it'd be easy to bond with him." He smiled at me and gave me a wink, but my thoughts were still on the warmth and the way I felt like every nerve on my body was charged from connecting with my queen. I could stay like this forever, I thought as my throat groaned again.

"How big?" The other seemed jealous of the comment on how large my kan were.

"The biggest I've ever seen," the other said with a shrug.

"Don't worm around, I'm serious... How big are they?" The warrior still kept his distance, probably still worried I did have the Molt Fever.

"I wasn't worming; they are the biggest I've seen."

"Does he have a scar on his chin?"

"What does it matter if he has a—"

"Does he?" the warrior interrupted. I was having trouble focusing on them, trying to keep the connection with my queen; the ebbing and flowing of her warmth was worrisome. Was something wrong with her? Was she injured? Did she need my help?

The warrior closest to me leaned in, and he didn't have to get so close to see the scar I held on my chin from the time I got cut by Prince Trent's ki stingers. They had been dripping with his black poison, and it had never healed properly. I should have died, but he wasn't the only one with poison in his veins. I just hadn't been as hasty to let my enemies know every trick up my skin. No one had tried to avoid my ki when I fought them. What was a cut but a temporary annoyance? But for Trent, well, people were more wary of being cut by him when I was the only one who had survived it. Many swear it was because the prince had not meant for him to die and must not have used his black death, but both of us knew better.

He respected me more after that, and I gave him my own respect in return for he had the best interests of the hive, and that was all that mattered.

"That's Commander Li-aq," the warrior said with worry. "Domsal has been looking for him. He's under her protection."

"So you're telling me that I shouldn't stick around to see if he needs my assistance?" He still joked about riding my dick. I was very particular about who I mated with and hadn't allowed myself to find my own klohvin within my warfleet, knowing that it would impede my judgment. My queen had promised me a mate that would help us grow a strong hive. She valued who I bonded with and made sure to remind me that I wasn't to waste my kantos on a random warrior in the hive. I was meant to lead and help restore our spawn. I would be a first mate to a queen, she would remind me. As she had already had a first mate long ago, I knew she was not talking of herself but of a future queen.

All I had to do was be patient. Having a klohvin was a risk to being a first mate to any female, so I avoided it.

With the queen's mind filling my own and my kan vibrating with need, I couldn't help the way I reached for the young warrior behind the neck and pulled him to me.

His lips pressed hard against mine, and I buzzed as they opened for me.

It seemed like the queen approved of my actions, and I heard her connection grow stronger as I deepened the kiss.

"I feel him," she said. "He will do nicely. Thank you for your offering. Bring me the other."

My kan touched the warrior's kan, and I moaned as I tossed him away from me. He stumbled back, lifting his fingers to his lips with a glazed look about him.

"Bapix," he called the hesitant warrior over.

"Did he musk you?" he asked while pacing uncomfortably.

"Bapix," he repeated in a husky tone that did not leave room for doubt about what he intended for Bapix when he got close enough.

"You know I'm not comfortable with things out in the open. I can't keep my musk under control," he said but the heave of resignation was proof that he would come to him regardless. "Just make sure that his dick stays on his side. I don't want him to wake up from his musk high and try to fight me for taking advantage. You can deal with that crap yourself."

I watched as Bapix was grabbed by the other warrior and their kan hooked onto each other until his eyes became milky and dull with the blessing of the queen.

It was as if the mating ceremony were in high swing, and the queen was connecting all three of us, but I had no desire to do anything but sit here in this resin hammock and enjoy the sensations washing over me.

"Jebinvol, do you feel her?" Bapix asked incredulously. "Is this Queen Mab?"

"No," I answered for him. Then my mouth went numb, but words still flowed feeling like sweet nectar on my tongue, "Bow to the future of the seven great hives. This is your king, and we will wait here for my queen to join us after her fun with her second mate."

"Am I not gracious? Am I not a queen of my honored word? Do not disappoint me, King Li-aq; this time when your queen is at your side, do not let her go. She is our future, and your spawn will revive the great hives!"

Pride filled my chest, and both my hearts thrummed as I lifted myself from the hammock with renewed strength. My wings snapped and stretched behind me as the warriors before me bowed low, their foreheads touching the ground. Was I a king? I wondered to myself, and the title felt right, like that was always what I was.

Would she admit that I was the lost spawn? That perhaps Gho-ran was not the last heir of Queen Kai?

"Queen mother?" I wondered if she would accept this honored title from me.

"You are the son I should have had," her voice caressed my mind with warmth and affection. "I searched many cycles to find your kantos, and when I did, you were the only one that responded to my touch. The others were unworthy of bringing the great hives back to Krelis."

My brothers and sisters were unworthy of the responsibility of the hive's future, I repeated to myself. I knew at that moment as the queen's warmth filled me that whatever spawnmates I had were gone. I was all that was left of the kantos stores from the hive I was from. Queen Kai was right. I was a king... not a prince as her own sons were. I was all that was left of what was once a great hive, and Queen Kai had saved me.

Xokol's words surfaced in my mind. "You are all that is left of Queen Sarak, and if you claim your place, many will follow."

Yes, I thought, as was right. They will follow when I've claimed my queen and the black star leads them to the future of Krelis.

Chapter Fifteen
Gaven

We shouldn't be staying in one place for too long until we could get back to Gho-ran, but all of my training went out the window when it came to my mate. She needed water, and the falls were the opposite direction of where we needed to go. The drip, drip, drip of the horrible filtration system would have to suffice until we knew whom we could trust in the hive.

Keep moving, my mind kept pestering me to leave, but as Ashley closed her eyes on my chest, I felt her slump from exhaustion. She held a similar weight to my own. Lives of the lost haunted her soul, and it felt as if the moment I told her I suffered the same, with the advice Loric had given me, the tension in her shoulders eased. A lightness filled me, and I eased her down on the bedding.

Staying here to let her rest wasn't an option if I wanted to reach a future together.

I allowed the loh on my legs to heat and form curved blades on my thighs. Wrapping them with membrane to protect the gorn from being punctured, I took the partially filled gorn of murky water. It would still have some nectar properties in it, but it was as clean as it would be going through the makeshift filtration I had hastily made for my mate. If I didn't run into any trouble, it was possible I could get us to a better source of water by the time she woke. Using a large cut of the membrane from the walls, the gorn was easily wrapped up and tied to my thigh loh, and then I picked up my goddess to leave.

She nuzzled into my hold, and I smiled with a warmth I never thought I'd get to feel.

"Gaven," she whispered my name on her lips.

"Hmm," I prompted just in case she wished to say something, and it wasn't simply that I was part of her dreams, a thought that brought pride to my heart. She was wearing her krelin horn adornment, and I enjoyed how her voice echoed in my implant. Somehow it connected our communications and made me feel like this was how krelins felt being part of the hive. She was my home.

"I'm not the black star," she confessed like I hadn't already dismissed the prophecies as merely the desperation of a species having trouble reproducing just as ours was.

"I wouldn't let them have you, even if you were."

There was truth in my words. I'd let the whole hive struggle to find a new prophecy of hope and revival because this goddess was mine.

I could feel her lips turn up in a smile against my skin. My own confession had pleased her.

"My mother would hate you," she said with a fondness for this information that I somehow understood.

"My Almder would feel the same if she knew I was stealing you for myself."

"Is that what you're doing?" she asked with a yawn, but when I glanced down, her dark eyes stared back at me.

Before I could reply, she hushed me with a finger to my lips, and she turned her head to the side, glancing around. I couldn't hear any krelin nearby; they weren't usually a stealthy species... unless it was Li-aq. My loh were still cracked and sore from our last encounter, though healing reasonably well. Humans might have perceptions that I did not, so I banked her worry and pushed my loh from my back to block us from a krelin's ability to sense our location with their kan. I wasn't sure how much longer my loh would still be able to keep expending energy without returning to the moons or absorbing some tarnpul, but I would push myself to make sure she was safe.

Just as I thought it, as if the goddess was listening and thought to punish me for taking what wasn't mine, my loh flickered and burned. I flinched and felt liquid drip down my shoulder blades. Tightening my jaw to push through the pain, I kept them going to keep our location hidden, but I knew hiding us like I had before was too much to ask without seeing a healer.

She finally spoke, distracted with whatever caught her attention. "Indi says that the whole planet is connected to nanotechnology that has enhanced the natural abilities of the indigenous species. All I have to do is find a working tablet, or..." Who was this Indi she spoke of? Ashley lifted a brow as she touched behind my ear where my implant was. A smile widened across her face in a devious manner that had my cock stirring once more. "Your implant isn't damaged like mine is, is it?"

"I've been assured the tarnpul casing would prevent erosion from my radiation," I answered, but added my concern about using it for communications while in the mountain. "My implant doesn't have the range of a normal communication unit, not while in the mountains and not with a tarnpul dampener surrounding it."

"Do you trust me?"

"With my life," I said with no hesitation. She was my mate, even if she had stabbed me in my sleep, I would simply make sure I removed possible weapons from where we slept. My life was hers to take.

"I'm not sure why our implants are connected when mine is so fucked up, but if yours isn't broken, then..." she pressed her fingers behind my ear and probed around until I felt a prick into my skin. "There we go; this is why jewelry is a lifesaver. I've inserted a wired needle into your implant. I keep it in the ring, just in case I want to fry someone's implant, but it can be used the other way too." She mumbled a phrase that didn't make sense in my ear, and I could see the blinking icon in my contact lens that notified me of a connection.

"You are getting slow with your aging years, Wizard. I was expecting you to receive my message much sooner," a teasing voice echoed in my implant.

"Indi, this is Gaven, though you already knew that."

"It is for the benefit of our temporary communicator, yes. I wasn't expecting you to keep him conscious, but I can see his vitals are still intact, though in need of some repair," the voice replied through my implant. I could see that he did not care that I was listening, nor was he speaking directly to me.

"What do you mean in need of repair?" She glared at me, and I wasn't sure if she was asking me or this Indi for details about my current health conditions. I wasn't about to admit to her that I was running on fumes. I would make it to the ship to secure her safety, and that's all that mattered.

"Your tone suggests that you were not aware and, therefore, not the cause of his injuries," Indie stated in assessment before continuing to answer. "Ah, this is why he is conscious. You wish to add him to the crew."

"Report!" Ashley got impatient with the voice.

"His radiation is at a dangerous level for his species, and multiple injuries have been identified with borrowed nanotechnology surrounding you both. I will run out of nanobots within your area if I proceed to evaluate his condition further. What radiation remains on him is destroying the nanobots at a rapid rate. They become damaged so easily, and I must maintain the connection with this implant to lead you back to the ship. I've instructed the nanobots surrounding you to keep their distance but remain close enough to relay our messages."

"You're hurt..." Ashley narrowed her eyes.. "How far are we from the ship? How quickly can you get us out of here?" She was asking the male on the other end of the communication. An urge to remind her that, though I would not stop her from having another mate for offspring, I would not allow him to have her after his duty was completed.

"The nanobots have a targeted sequencing in line with our mission and have limited memory to rewrite commands. Their primary functions are communication to update commands and blocking the replication sequences of bio-organisms. This means they are capable of sensing biomaterial health to make sure their jobs are accomplished and assist with us talking now. I do not have your location, but I can relay if you're getting closer based on the strength of our connection."

"Is it reversible?" she asked, speaking of whatever job the nanobots were doing while on Krelis.

"When I rewrote the code to sense the estreld's health condition, it triggered a self-destructive sequencing. Hijacking their communication link is simple and does not disrupt their main objectives. However, if I touch any other code, the nanobot only lasts a few seconds before it burns up. I believe there is a passcode we are missing to alter the virus."

"Was there a prompt in the code when you hacked it?" she asked, and that's when I heard the clicking sounding through the halls. Someone was using their kan to sense their surroundings. There was a distinct way they used their throat when talking and when simply using the vibration to help their kan "see" more. They were searching, the sound echoing in a steady pulse, timed and targeted. My radiation would keep us hidden for a time, but I didn't have enough to cloak us if they got closer. They would see us if we came across them.

"That would be too easy," Indi joked. "The nanobot is created like an organism. There are no prompts or any obvious intentions for modifications to the original code, but the way it reacted when changing the coding suggests that there is a sequence of approaching the technology that would allow for reprogramming."

While they were speaking, I picked up my pace through the halls, holding her closely. Being careful and slow with my movements made my cloaking more effective, but we were running out of time, and we didn't want to run into whoever was coming.

As we passed under a breeze, I glanced up to see the tunnel above us open, the membrane separating. Correction, we had no time. Many warriors didn't have implants with communicators. They learned the language they needed, and very few sacrificed their kan's strength by having technology interfering with that. Whoever Ashley connected with would not be able to track them through the hive if they couldn't even know our own location.

Her mouth opened, and I quickly pressed my lips to hers to stop her words. There wasn't enough radiation in me to block our sound waves. I didn't like the idea of being trapped in a room to hide when I couldn't keep us cloaked.

We were surrounded.

Our choices vanished. We could either hide in a room or run into a warrior whose loyalties I didn't know. It was unusual to have so many searching like they did in a hunting unit. The way the clicking echoed was similar to how they scanned through their warships after I had found an illegal harvesting nest.

It was my job to stop the nests from forming to keep our fragile alliance functioning. If the clan knew what krelins did to our species, they would call for war, and we would starve with the trade dried up.

But here I was in the center of their hive and nearly drained as they surrounded us. My heart raced, pounding against my chest with anxiety and fear I hadn't felt in a long time. Not for myself. I knew what I had signed up for with the missions I was assigned. Making it back to the clan was never a certainty, but with my mate in my arms... her species didn't survive long on Krelis. Trusting Gho-ran, Mabel or Trent was one of common interest, but I never spoke to any of them about the things

I'd seen, the decay that was left in their hive from their fallen queen's poison roots.

Setting Ashley down, I unlatched the gorn from my thigh and handed it to her before peeling back the membrane of the room we were next to.

"I'll make a path," I assured her.

"What?"

The other male's voice was still in my implant, speaking to me now, "Gaven, I'm picking up on approximately ten krelins targeting your location based on the pitch of what I've researched is called the saling, the act of feeling the land through their kan with the assistance of practiced throat vibrations."

"Indi, he doesn't need a dictionary," Ashley chided. "Have you disabled your personality download?"

"I'm not a robot," he denied and clipped back, "My personality is not simply disabled. I choose when to use it and wondering whether I can trust this Gaven to finish Mission Wizard in his current condition is troubling. There is a low probability that he can push through the incoming ten krelin warriors to make a path for you even if he threw his body in the way as a distraction."

"Personality intact then," Ashley said with a sigh. "Ignore him." She was talking to me now, and I was still moving up ahead, hearing them both through my implant.

I readied my arm loh into curved blades and pushed out my loh from my shoulders to protect myself from how some krelins liked to stab from above with the talons on the ends of the wings. Gritting my teeth, I pushed through the pain at overusing my loh.

The tap of footsteps came behind me, but they were much too soft for a krelin boot. Glancing over my shoulder, I found it was Ashley, following in my wake.

"No one is skewering themselves against the krelins without me. You're going to stop running and walk normally." She sounded agitated with me and then glared before demanding, "Stop. Right now!"

I did as she asked, and I heard the buzz of krelin wings up ahead and heavier footfalls from the direction we had just come from. Ashley huffed from trying to catch up to my large strides, and still carrying the gorn, she lifted it to her mouth and drank.

"Gah," she coughed and wiped at her mouth with her arm, a wrinkle forming at the bridge of her nose. "Fuck, what is this shit?" She pointed ahead of us and shouted at the krelins, "You call this nectar?"

"Not every krelin has a translator," I told her, seeing the way she was intentionally getting their attention.

"Doesn't matter," she said with a shrug and shook the gorn at them. "You're going to keep your promise, right?"

"Which one?" I watched as her ass made the flaps of her krelin attire swish, and I could see that beautiful crease where her thighs and her ass met. I licked my lips becoming distracted with the way she swayed her hips like a mating dance. "I keep all my promises."

"Good," she clipped with a wink back at me. "Because if this doesn't work, then you're going to have to fix yourself up and go get my team from the ship."

Which promise was she talking about?

"Don't let them keep me," she said before the first krelin approached and she tossed the gorn at them. Quick reflexes had her grabbing the gorn, and she sniffed it, checking for any explosives or simply confused by the subtle smell of most of the nectar being filtered out to water.

"It smells unfinished," she said to the other warriors.

"Hand it here," he offered. Then she gave him the gorn.

He sniffed it and then took a gulp, sputtering when he tasted it. "It's disgusting," he agreed.

"There are other gorns; that one was probably peed in as a joke," the third teased, and the one who drank it was now spitting on the ground.

"I'm glad we found you," the female said. "You are the black star, yes? The huemoon that will lead us to the great hives. Domsal said you were taken while recovering from fever."

"What about the other one?" another warrior hissed.

"He looks like he could use some help," she said dismissively and focused on Ashley, "We have a celebration prepared for you if you'll allow Motvek to fly you to the heart of the hive. I'm told that you can understand us. Our translators don't have your tongue installed yet, but everyone that has one will be ready by tonight. Motvek is highly skilled in creating beautiful clothes and repairing the ones you have."

The other three behind her bowed to me and moved to block any escape. The leer in one of their eyes told me everything I needed to know. He stared at my loh with dilated interest. It was unclear if all of them were part of a harvest nest, but as he got closer, I could make out the tattooed crystals along the inside of his arm. He had four confirmed kills of my clan, and that didn't count how many he might have been directly involved in kidnapping for their butchery.

Whatever my mate's plan was, I saw blue seeing those tattoos. When the krelin got close enough, my face revealing nothing, I grabbed his wrist to prevent his stinger from releasing and plunged my loh blade up under his ribs. He slumped against my shoulder, plunging his neck into my blades there as I whispered in his ear before he faded, "This was a mercy."

He should have died slowly, but I did not have the time to allow him to feel what he made my clan feel as he had peeled their loh from their flesh, still alive to keep them potent after extraction.

My mate had a curious smile on her face as she screamed and ran into the arms of the female warrior. The warrior didn't notice as she gathered her up and didn't see her lift her ring to behind her ear to jam a needle with focused precision.

There wasn't a question in her eyes about why I had done what I had done. She simply made the best of the situation and acted on it.

My chest swelled with pride and gratitude that she would not curse me for ruining her plans with my rash behavior.

Twisting my hold on the traitor in my arms, I blocked the other warrior from clawing at me. His talons slashed down his fellow warrior's back, cutting through his wings. There was no scream of pain from my shield; he had already returned to the great rock; his blood pooled down my shoulder and coated my chest and back, a sickly purple color, thick and sticky on my skin. Their blood smelled like their nectar, or I should say their nectar smelled like their blood, a sweet and pungent fume that I knew would trigger a calming and disorientating effect if I let any of it seep into my mouth or my wounds. The blood tingled on my loh, and I knew my time was limited before I allowed my guard to slip.

Removing my loh blade from the dead krelin's gut to toss his weighted body at the next warrior coming at me gave me time to lunge, and I blasted a surge of radiation through my back loh before the other could grab me from behind. There were screams and you could feel the pain in the air. My mate's scream was forced for show, and she wasn't that great of an actor because they sounded like she was taking my cock, and I felt myself harden inside my mating loh as if she were calling for me to please her.

The female warrior screamed as she clutched at her head and fell to her knees. I'd seen a similar reaction when I had used my radiation to short out implants in former skirmishes. I grinned through the blood of my enemies knowing, somehow, she had destroyed the implant and given herself the advantage to knee the warrior in the skull, knocking him out in a heap at her feet. It was a beautiful sight that had me stirring for her, and that was exactly what I had planned when I was finished with the rest of these annoyances between me and my mate.

Ducking under and spinning around through the blood was a rush. My blade opened the krelin's throat, and all I had eyes for was my mate as she watched me. The krelin behind me was still screaming as its scales melted and skin bubbled from the focused use of my loh. My knees trembled, as my vision blurred, but I wouldn't stop until I reached her. Until I made sure she was safe.

Two more krelins came at me, and I roared, fighting against the fatigue of radiation depletion. They took to the air, their wings buzzing in my ears. The other two remaining krelins tried to corner me on the ground. Four against one.

I stood there, lifting a brow, and with a twisted grin I waited for them.

"He's not even bending the sky," one of them commented to the others. She was able to notice their advantage over me, that my radiation was too low to disappear before their eyes and reappear to murder them without them ever seeing what had happened.

"He'd have used it by now," the one in the air agreed.

With more confidence, they closed in on me, and I thought, just a little closer. The female krelin clucked her throat in a warcry, and I didn't even turn to defend. The male in front of me lunged, and he didn't think I'd counter by going towards them. They expected me to duck with the krelins flying above, but I jumped to use the krelin in front of me like a stepping stone, reaching to grab the boots of the krelin above.

The sudden weight of me shocked the krelin, and he was unable to keep his flight. Yanking on his boot, I pulled him beneath me as we tumbled to the ground, crunching his wings in a way that I knew he wouldn't be flying again during our current duel.

I couldn't be sure that these remaining krelin were part of whatever harvest nest the other was involved in, but with my mate here, I couldn't risk that they were just the gatherers and not the butchers of my clan.

Guilty by association, I thought as I pressed my curved blade into the throat of the krelin I had rolled on top of, ending our tumble with my loh heating to slice through his neck like lard. His head rolled from his shoulders.

"Nooo!" the female behind me screamed; the pain in her cry told of her attachment to this male, more so than the one I had taken care of first or the other I had burned up after that.

Her awareness of the situation was lost to her senses as emotion ruled her next moves. The warrior pulled out a dagger made of many stingers gathered together from a sheath at her thigh. Females didn't have stingers, or ki, as the krelins called them. She must have gathered them from her fallen warriors as a tribute to them to still have their ki honor the hive in battle.

From the corner of my eye, I saw my mate move towards us to help, but I shook my head, hoping to dissuade her.

If she got too close, I couldn't use the last push of my radiation to end this duel.

The glow of my loh flickered in preparation. Three krelins charged, one from the air, one from behind, and the other rolled from being stepped on and was only seconds behind his comrades. It was good enough, I thought.

Bent on one knee, crouched over the corpse of my last kill, I prepared to move.

The female reached me first, and I didn't trust that the ki dagger she held wasn't poisoned. I didn't wish to kill more of them, but I'd accepted that was the result after my loh had gutted the first one.

My loh blasted with radiation, and all I had to do was stand as I watched the female and the male too close to me scream as their scales melted, sliding from their flesh. Their scales were hardy and would not melt, but that didn't stop the skin around them from being damaged. Their leathers stayed intact as well, telling me that they had used estreld's loh to reinforce them. Too bad for them that it didn't save the parts of them not covered.

Through the heat, I knew the last krelin would be disorientated, unable to see where I was within the blast. My hand shot out and gripped him by the throat; my other gripped his wrist to prevent his ki from stabbing me.

My vision narrowed on his golden eyes, and I squeezed his throat as I demanded answers. "Tell me where your harvest nest is, and I may spare your life."

I wouldn't. If he knew anything about the nest, I would kill him. If he knew nothing, I would give him a quick death.

His horns were too small for him to stab me without considerable effort to counter the hold I had on him. His wings could be used to throw us off balance, but shock prevented him from thinking clearly.

"Dom-sss—" he began to say before I heard the gasp of my mate.

The voice of her friend in my implant repeated in my mind, "Ten."

Ten krelins were detected by one called Indi.

I processed through the kills mentally.

The first was the one with the tattoo of a butcher as I gutted him.

The second, I had cut through their throat as I twisted to reach the other.

The third, my mate had taken care of.

The fourth, I had burned their face, their screams fading as they crumbled to the ground as I had stabbed the fifth.

Four krelins, two on the ground, two in the air. Beheaded, burned, burned, and the one in my grip as my fist closed on his throat.

That was only nine, I thought with horror.

My eyes flicked over to where she was, and then the unfinished confession of the male that bled from his mouth as I twisted his own stinger into his chest came together in my mind.

The old female krelin that had been a caretaker to Gho-ran, saved his life, and my own on several occasions smiled at me before she... kissed my mate?

Domsal.

My knees gave out as I swayed from my radiation being spent. The krelin fell to the ground with me, and I shoved him to the side as I clawed forward trying to reach my mate. My legs wouldn't work, and I dug my arm loh into the ground to pull my weight.

"Skybender," she tutted as she approached. She left my mate behind her, not even trying to detain her. Was I wrong? Is she safe? Can Domsal be trusted?

My mate simply stood behind her, staring down at me with a lifted brow. Something felt wrong, off.

"Goddess?" I questioned as I reached for her.

"Gho-ran will be so disappointed that you've put yourself in such a state," Domsal said with an exhausted sigh. "I'm not surprised," she spoke in the human tongue, "The hive has forgiven you for your crimes because of the pardons Gho-ran insisted on and Queen Mab's favor, but this I cannot ignore. These warriors came to help protect and celebrate the Black Star. They meant no harm to either of you."

Domsal turned to my mate and asked her, "What are your thoughts, My Queen? Should we patch him up and send him on the first transport back to his planet or bring him to trial? I know Gho-ran would prefer we allow him to live."

Ashley shook her head, and pity filled her eyes as she stepped forward to gaze upon my pitiful form. My head couldn't lift itself any longer, and my cheek slumped into a pool of blood from one of the fallen warriors I'd slain.

"His judgment isn't mine to give. Only the goddess can grant his soul's release. All of our hands are dirty from death. Bring him to the heart of the hive."

You are my goddess, I thought staring up at her through heavy lids, my vision blurring. Only your absolution will heal my soul. Nothing else mattered.

"My life is yours," I said with a final tremor before my eyes closed.

Chapter Sixteen

Ashley

"Go to him!" I screamed, but no words left my mouth. My lips still tingled from that bitch with the same name I'd heard Indi say was who had bought my contract to the slut shack.

Domsal, the name whispered through my implant from Gaven's lips as he tried to pull himself across the floor.

"Why aren't you doing anything?" I thought I asked but couldn't hear the echo of my voice beyond my mind. Suddenly, my vision expanded to take in my surroundings.

Blood splattered across the membrane walls; pools of purple gathered around the bodies strewn across the large cavern. I watched as one of the bodies twitched and stretched the membrane of an opening in the floor. The flesh was melting from their face, and they tumbled down the hole that tore through the ground. Their wing got caught in the thick lining, and they suspended until the talon of their wing ripped at the seam, and they fell.

Then my eyes caught on the head tilted against their horn, keeping them from rolling from their body, covered in purple fluid with their mouth slack from death. The smell in the air was sweet like warmed honey mixed with charred meat. My stomach churned.

I'd seen death but not like this.

Bodies were everywhere, and then my eyes landed on Gaven, and my brow rose with confusion. He had done this, I knew that. I planned on confusing and tricking the krelins into taking us both to the ships, but then he had attacked them.

At the time, I had gone with it and tried to fight our way to freedom, but now that I had time to process the information...

Why?

Why had he done it?

Domsal's words caught my attention. "I cannot ignore this..." None of these krelins had been sent to kill us. I stared at the krelin with their throat cut and remembered the warrior at my feet had said he was an excellent tailor and would fix my clothes as well as create something beautiful for me for the celebration of finding me, someone they thought was from prophecy.

I may not have wanted to be their prophet, but they weren't here to kill us. I hadn't killed the female unconscious on the ground. She'd wake with a horrible headache from her implant being overloaded and the knee to the face, but she'd be fine. She twitched on the ground, reassuring me she was alive.

"Goddess?" Gaven's voice trembled.

Domsal asked me what we should do with him for his crimes, and I was at a loss, but words came to me then with ease. It wasn't my place to judge him. The krelins and the estrelds believed in a goddess, though they called her something different.

"Let the goddess judge him," I had thought to myself, the words warm in my mind like I was talking to myself.

I didn't want to leave him here to die.

Domsal nodded, lowering her head to me in a bow. "We will bring him then to be heard by the hive. I'll have the warriors brought to your Kloaph Rites for their journey to the goddess."

She was speaking in English, so I didn't have the echo of my translator, which was nice. I wasn't afraid of the old krelin. She didn't appear that old, but her voice was gravelly from use, and there was a milkiness to her eyes that spoke of sight loss. I knew she wasn't young despite her dark hair and strong stance.

"Kloaph?" I didn't understand the word, but as soon as I said it, I could hear a whisper, "Mating Bond."

"I'm being mated?" I questioned, further feeling my mind again answer for me, "Only if I found him worthy."

Warmth filled my chest, and an ache squeezed my insides as I watched Gaven's eyes close with a whisper I could hear echoed in my implant. We were still connected.

"My life is yours."

Were we really the same as I thought? He had killed these krelins with a smile on his face, and I had a plan to get us out of this without bloodshed. Even if they took me, he promised he wouldn't let them keep me as their prophet. Hadn't I known what that promise meant to a guy like him?

Was I responsible for these deaths?

It wouldn't be the first time, I thought with regret. Here was the woman who had purchased my contract, but she didn't restrain me, and even with her hive slaughtered around her, she didn't try to finish the one who had taken their lives. She asked what I thought we should do with him and accepted it.

Perhaps being a prophet meant more than I thought it did to them. She called me queen and didn't kill him while he was unconscious or try to force me to follow her.

"Will he live?" I asked her.

"Estrelds are hard to kill. If he returns to his planet, he would heal quickly, but here on krelis... we had stores of tarnpul that held his moon's radiation that would have helped him, but those were loaded onto our warships to help the estrelds join the coming war against the outlaws on their way to this sector of the universe."

My heart beat faster with anxiety, but my body wouldn't move to gather him into my arms. She sensed my alarm and patted my arm in an effort to soothe me.

"Gho-ran keeps some tarnpul in his quarters. He has a soft spot for the estreld, and we have healers who can make sure he is stable for a trip back to his planet. I've already sent word to the closest warriors to join us here. They'll be here shortly."

"You have?"

She smiled, but it didn't reach her eyes. She touched my head and then her own. "Our kan can send distress signals. The hive knows we need help."

"Our kan..." Right, I was wearing the headband with krelin horns on them. It felt wrong to be wearing them as we were surrounded by death. I reached to remove them but stopped myself.

"It is an honor to wear them."

I shouldn't disrespect the hive by removing them right now unless they asked me to. I was responsible for the deaths in this cavern, but Domsal looked on me with kindness in her golden eyes. I was the monster here, not them.

I knelt in the pool of blood next to Gaven and touched his cheek. It was cold, no longer warm like I remembered him as he made me forget for a moment what kind of life I had signed up for. Sliding down his neck, there was still a pulse, slow but steady. He was alive.

The buzz of wings echoed from the ceiling. Several krelins entered the cavern, and they roared at the loss of their fallen.

Bodies were recovered, stacked atop each other. One took a net folded up at their thigh and placed it on the ground. Then another did the same, making the net bigger. One by one the dead were gently placed on the net; even the one beheaded had his skull placed where it would have attached. The edges of the net were brought together and all eight bodies bundled up tightly.

Finally, someone spoke to break the silence, "Return to the hive." My eyes snapped from the bodies to the one whose voice I remembered. He was the one who helped break my fever with the weird gua bugs.

They all gathered around the net, and they knelt down to palm the pool of blood at their feet. Cupping the blood, each brought the blood to their lips and drank in some kind of death ritual. When they finished, they licked their palms and then smeared the blood on their chests. With pursed lips they spit, and strings were pulled from their mouth that they attached to the net.

The one I remembered took a step back and allowed the krelins to push from the ground into the air. Each of their strings attached to the net and with their combined efforts lifted the net of eight warriors.

He then approached me with a shake of his head. He was disappointed but said, "I'm glad you are unharmed. Would you allow me the honor of preparing you for your Kloaph, and we will mourn their deaths by allowing them to leave this life through the spawning of a new hive?"

He knelt at my dirtied feet and gently placed his horns against my stomach. He could skewer me with those large weapons, but he was careful, and I felt my stomach hum with the contact. Warmth spread through my belly and made my fingers tingle.

"Accept his generosity," I heard myself encourage, and my hands reached out to grab his horns. Kan, I reminded myself. These were kan. He shivered at my touch, and I smiled at the power they placed with me.

Two other warriors took each end of Gaven and followed after the net of death up into the hive tunnels.

As I watched them leave, I squeezed the kan in my hands, and the krelin moaned. He can't leave without me; I ached as Gaven disappeared, but how could I support what had happened in this cavern at his hands?

"He's being brought to the ceremony. He'll be stabilize,d and you can decide what to do with him then," his deep voice brought my attention back, and I released his horns, allowing him to stand. He was a large krelin, and his wings whipped out, sending a delicious aroma in the air. He smelled like winter. I liked winter, I thought absently.

"What is that amazing smell?"

"I'm glad you like it," he said with a grin.

"King Li-aq," Domsal bowed her head, "my Queen has told me that Gho-ran will have his own hive after he earns his place from leading our fleets to victory against the coming war. Once she revealed who you were, I understand now that I was wrong in doubting her. Please forgive me."

"There is nothing to forgive. Everything is how it should be. The goddess has given us our path, and we will follow her brightest star." He didn't take his black eyes from me, and I watched as they took on a violet glow, different from what I'd seen of other krelins. His hand lifted and traced through my hair until I knew they ran over the small kan I was wearing. "As it should be," he repeated.

"I don't understand," I said but didn't know if I actually said it or only thought it, but Domsal explained regardless.

"The prophecy of a queen brought back from death makes sense now," she agreed. "The one to wear her kan is meant to be the mate of a lost king. I thought it was Gho-ran, but I didn't consider the other lost hives."

"He is ours," I thought, and then I told him, "It's time."

A small voice whispered underneath my curiosity to see what the krelin did at a Kloaph Ceremony. That made me shiver. "Mate, you promised..."

I blinked and stared at the formidable krelin as he spread his wings and offered his hand. I didn't believe in fucking prophecies, I thought with an irritated scowl, nor did I believe in being destined to some alien mate. But I couldn't deny that he hadn't shown me anything but kindness, and he wasn't quick to kill someone who had slaughtered eight krelins who weren't showing signs of hostility.

I didn't know what to think.

The female krelin that I had knocked out groaned on the ground, and I didn't want to be here when she finally woke. King Li-aq wrapped his arms around my waist and pulled me against him with a snap that made my breath catch. That sweet smell consumed me, and I found myself melting into it, sucking in more with a whimper.

"What the fuck is that smell?" I moaned but felt a bit sleepy as my vision narrowed, and I struggled to stay awake.

"I don't intend on being a second mate," he said with a growl; then his throat clucked, reminding me of crickets at night. It was almost like a song. He whispered so only I could hear past the buzz of his wings lifting us in the air, my hips pressed against him, "The hive can have everything from me, My Queen, but not this. My mate will be mine alone. And I won't have you otherwise. I don't give a fuck, as your tongue would say, what prophecy says about you. I will not settle for anything less than first and only to my queen."

Chapter
Seventeen
Gaven

T he way my mate glanced around at the carnage I had caused tore at my insides. I could be a monster in everyone's eyes but hers. I couldn't handle failing again, and that's what I'd done when she looked at me that way. Eyes full of questions and distrust.

I gasped awake, groaning, unable to move.

"Don't try moving, unless you'd care to bleed out. It's of no concern of mine," Li-aq's voice filtered through my ears, and I growled.

"Ashley, where is she?" I demanded.

"She isn't a prisoner if that's what you're asking. She's being prepared for our mating. I'm not an outlaw, hiding and taking what isn't his to claim," he said casually, insulting me as my eyes pried open to watch him grinning at me. I was wrapped up in krelin thread, and there were a few tarnpul rocks sitting on my chest.

"I wouldn't get any ideas about escaping from that resin. It's the only thing keeping you conscious in the state you're in."

"Where is she?" I didn't believe him that she was willingly choosing this male to mate with.

"She's not banned from seeing you, Skybender. She's a queen; she can do as she pleases. I'm not here to keep you company."

"Why are you here, then?" I snapped.

"Now we're asking the right questions," he said pleased with himself, and I wanted to rip my loh into his smug face. "I want you to return to Estreldez, heal yourself up, and never return to Krelis. I'm keeping you alive because I don't believe she would appreciate killing you in my Kloaph Rites, but tradition would dictate that, if I don't accept you as klohvin or a second mate, which I don't, I'm to duel you and feed your hearts to my mate."

He sighed. "Right, you do not have two hearts, but just the one would do if you don't wish to leave to save yourself."

"I will duel," I told him, and he laughed.

"You are in no condition to be a worthy opponent, and I can't show you mercy with the hive watching."

183

"I will duel all the same. Just give me a radiation pack and allow me to eat some glorbin flower. I know you have some."

He lifted a brow. "Glorbin flower is hard to come by."

"You have some," I repeated.

"And you eat it," he shook his head, but I could see the way his lip twitched with curiosity before trying to press my buttons again, "Estrelds eat hewve shit; who am I to deny your last meal?"

We used glorbin flower as a seasoning, crushed up and used rarely. It was difficult to mine, and estrelds have died in the caves to retrieve it, but if they do find it... it has saved lives. Even Mabel had a time when she was an offspring when she had to take a pinch of glorbin dust with her meals to get the nutrients she needed before the imports of nectar helped regulate her health.

Countless times, I'd returned to the clan on the fumes of glorbin flower alone, near death, and it sustained me until I could recover under the moon's glow.

"I'll have it delivered, but if you use it to kill more of my warriors, you won't make it to the Rakin, and your heart will be fed to my mate as she rides my cock."

He was baiting me, and he thought only he could play that game. I grinned at him as I told him, "I've been spying on you for countless cycles. You're no more fertile than I am, and if you get near my mate without her consent, I'll make sure you never will be."

I'd burn off his cock and feed it to him in a melted soup that would sear down his throat like the lava that flowed beneath this mountain.

His throat clicked with irritation, and he musked the room, making me sleepy. He could have killed me, but I'd known Li-aq for longer than our current predicament. I had been prepared to die killing him at the orbiting station... neither of us was dead yet.

As my vision narrowed, I watched as the black veins along his arms pulsed, confirming my suspicions. He was a hotheaded krelin, and I didn't make promises I wouldn't keep. If he touched my mate, I would destroy him. But I knew now, when he thought I wasn't conscious enough to remember, he could have killed me and many others without even trying too hard. One nick was all it would have taken.

We still didn't know a cure for the black death. Regular krelin poison could be burned through with enough radiation, but the black veins were a rare trait of the kind of poison that couldn't be cured with fever.

The fucker was deadly but hadn't used it like the Prince of Krelis had regularly. Every duel, you could see his black veins pulse, a warning to reconsider challenging him, but Li-aq... he had the same poison, but this was the first time it'd been verified by sight. Not once in all of his battles had he used it. Not that anyone knew of.

He was either the most prideful of warriors and more dangerous than anyone would have guessed, or he was more in control than he seemed and one of the most merciful of his species.

Only time would tell which he was. Perhaps he was both.

Chapter
Eighteen
Ashley

"We look beautiful," I told myself as I glanced into polished glass and stroked my horn adornment with a smile.

My mate is waiting for me, I thought, and I frowned at myself with confusion. When I thought of Li-aq, he appeared surrounded in green smoke, and then purple blood splattered everywhere, and I shuttered.

Leathers were draped down my back in vibrant colors, and I stared at the greens in the design. My arms lifted up, the leather fanning out like wings. The dress I wore was made up of multiple cuts of leather layered like tiny pebbles, intricately weaved like a second skin. I turned to the side to admire the way it curved and molded to me, and my skin glistened at the small swell of my breasts exposed at the open seam.

"The hive has gathered at the heart, My Queen," Domsal prompted, and I nodded.

It felt like I was missing something, and I stalled in front of the mirrored glass, trying to figure out what it was, but all I felt was my gut twisting in on itself. My nerves were on fire.

Domsal reassured me, "It's normal to be nervous at your Kloaph. I'm still hopeful that Gho-ran will be able to return in time to see how magnificent you are, but he will understand your choice to revive the Sarak Hive."

I nodded. Krelis needed me, and Li-aq was kind and handsome.

My implant made my ear tingle, and I rubbed at it.

"Wizard, are you there?" It was Indi, and I smiled at the familiar voice, but it was faint and crackled like the connection was experiencing interference.

"Not now, Indi," I whispered. "I'm about to be mated."

"I thought you already were," he said, "Nevermind, bring him with you. The team has seen activity at the volcano's venting system."

"An eruption?" I asked, concerned.

Domsal lifted a brow ridge and questioned, "My Queen, are you well?"

"No, the krelins maintain the magma swells. I see no indication of an eruption, but increased krelin activity shows they are gathering." His voice crackled like an old radio, "If you can get to the vent, the air is hot enough to be used to be lifted from the volcano where the ship can grab you. Chester has been sent down with the equipment for you both to escape. I'll be waiting."

And then he was gone, leaving me in confusion.

There was no reason to escape, the krelins would do anything I asked of them. I hadn't been given the chance to tell Indi I was fine before he disconnected, but I was relieved I would get to see Chester again.

Moisture pooled at my eyes, the relief so palpable to know he was alive, and I just knew that meant Bryce was too. My team was okay.

Li-aq waited for me outside the room and smiled when he saw me. "You are a goddess," he said, and I got this sinking feeling in the pit of my belly. His eyes were violet, but I, for a brief moment, thought they were green. I shook the haze from my head.

He flew me through the hive until we reached the large heart of the krelins where the mountain opened up to the sky, and the heat from the planet's core gusted up from the center. Krelins floated in the air, ebbing and soaring, some using their wings, and others had clothes like mine to ride the natural wave of the heated air. The winged leather tied to my wrists floated up,

189

taking up some of the wind, and my heels lifted from the ledge. The drop below appeared endless, but a krelin netting sucked up and down with the gusts.

I glanced up in awe at the several platforms layered from here all the way to the cresting of the sky meeting the mountain. Krelins bounced from one platform to the next using the constant flow of hot air, and some stayed flying with their wings flapping so fast that they disappeared at certain angles.

"Magnificent, isn't it?" Li-aq stepped off the ledge and expanded his wings. He put out his hand to prompt me to join him, but I hesitated, glancing down at the drop below us. Then I twisted the ring on my finger, back and forth, feeling the needle within it extend and retract with a soft click.

The krelins could sense his arrival, and all of them floated off to the sides where the ledges tiered throughout the volcanic opening. Clicking noises sounded throughout the large space, echoing, and my translator couldn't pinpoint any one singular conversation to translate. It became nothing more than white noise that made my head throb. Trusting the krelins, I stepped off the ledge, and my makeshift wings and my gorgeous dress captured the air, sending me floating upwards. My hand slipped within Li-aq's, and he flew us through the heart, as they called it, and landed us on one of the larger platforms that took up a large section of the vent. As my feet reached over the platform, my weight tugged me down, only eased by the hold Li-aq had on my hand. The dead warriors were hanging from the ledge above this one like sick ornaments held together with resin and thread. I was beginning to think the krelins had a lot in common with spiders with how they preserved things. I covered my mouth to hold back my bile, but a voice inside me thought calmly, "They will be remembered. This is how we honor the dead." I'd hate to think of how they honored the living... but I was about to find out, wasn't I? The female warrior who had been there when they died was narrowing her eyes at me, but she stayed beside her fallen, guarding them.

"Do not worry about Pironsa," Li-aq patted my hand. "She is not upset that you destroyed her implant. She is upset because you did not allow her the honor of dying with her unit. She knows you saved her life, but as she was the general, she believes she could have changed the result, and if she couldn't, then she deserved to join them. It is normal survivor's guilt, and I am grateful to you for sparing her as she will be needed when the outlaws come.

"Come, you will grant her first honors in tonight's celebration before I take you to the sacred grounds of Goddess Lenkal where we will have many cycles to bond and re-emerge as one."

"How do I do that?"

"Give Pironsa first honor or slide upon my cock until you can hear me inside your soul."

I sputtered, and he chuckled, "As I've said before, My Queen, I will not mate you without first proving myself worthy. We have time. The Kai Mountains are plentiful in everything we will need to stay there for many cycles and enjoy our Kloaph Rites."

Domsal floated up behind us and dropped more gracefully than I had to the platform. She didn't have wings, but she did have more experience with utilizing their clothing to the fullest.

"King Li-aq, you said you stayed with her until her fume fever broke, and you honored her request to not kill the one who murdered our warriors. I'd say you have already proven your worth to the hive and the queen, but I am from a different time. I cannot begin to understand all the ways of this generation. You are strong, handsome, and the last surviving spawn of Queen Sarak."

"Commander, My King," Pironsa addressed before reluctantly turning her attention to me and gritting, "Queen, I wish to be honored along with my unit."

Li-aq answered for me, "Don't be selfish. I would have been honored as such many times over if not for the next threat against the hive. And there is a threat against the hive, Pironsa. You are needed."

She clucked her throat in annoyance and rolled her shoulders back but nodded her understanding. "I will honor them and then join them after I have gifted them with the deaths of our enemies."

"That's a good girl," he approved and guided me to the edge to face the hive, my back to the warriors. "It's time to begin the celebration and show them hope for our future," he whispered to me while giving me a squeeze along my waist to show that he was here for me.

"And how am I supposed to do that?" I hissed back, crankier than I intended to be.

I glanced down to see a net being flown up to me by warriors. They held it taunt like they wanted me to step onto it.

My feet moved as if an invisible string pulled them forward, and I stepped on the net. The gust of the heated air was softer right now, only fluttering my leathers and making my toes practically float on the net, providing that stability to not fall to my death. The net carrying me drifted away from the security of the ledge, and even if I jumped I wouldn't reach. My life was in the hands of the krelins holding the net, their wings keeping us afloat when the flow of the volcanic vent wasn't gusting like it had been before. Li-aq waited at the platform with the warriors, and I was lifted to be seen by all of the krelins gathered.

The tension on the net wobbled with the weight of another krelin, and I stopped looking over my shoulder to see a beautiful white-haired krelin watch me with golden eyes. She had black horns following the curve of her skull and tucking under her ears through her white strands. Her leather wings must have been propped up with wires as they didn't float the same as mine did in the wind.

She watched me curiously and then smiled.

I was about to ask who she was, but she answered, "Who am I? I'm Queen Kai, and through you, my daughter will live."

I shook my head, but the voice returned stronger than a whisper in my head, "Witness, my warriors, the reborn queen! My Daughter of Prophecy to revive our great hives has come. She wears the kan, and I will share with you that she is one with the hive!"

"How can a hooman revive our great hives? They don't survive long here," I could hear someone say, but I didn't know where it was coming from.

"Queen Mab and Prince Trent are protecting our hive; we should await their return to bless this prophecy," another said. I darted my eyes around trying to figure out who was talking, but it was no use. The clicking of everyone's throats was too overwhelming.

I held my head, and then warmth filled my body like the sun was wrapping me up in a comforting hammock on a calm summer day. Earth, I thought with a smile, it felt like home.

"Come to me Panala," Queen Kai opened her arms. Who was Panala? Another krelin handed the queen a gorn, and she lifted it up above her head. "Open yourself," she commanded.

My knees grew weak, and I collapsed to the net below me, and another krelin buzzed next to me and lifted my chin to the queen as she pour the gorn's contents over me.

I choked and sputtered on the deep purple liquid that sloshed over me. The krelin that had lifted my chin pinched my cheeks to make sure I drank, and it overflowed from my lips and clogged up my airways as I gasped. A gust from below had the blood returning back up from the net to float around me in a morbid display. The wind caught on my clothes, and I floated up as I noticed the queen's wings weren't leather like mine; they were buzzing and moving like any other warrior's. I hadn't seen a single female warrior have wings, but she did.

Our eyes met, and it was like she saw through me; a twisted smile curled her lips. There was a large scar above her heart that had black veins running towards it like a curse. She tossed the gorn without a care for where it landed and reached out to cup my cheeks in her hands.

"You are ready to receive me, daughter."

Fuck, I thought with fear that surpassed the warmth that filled my body.

I could hear my own mother's voice in my head, "Death follows you, and if you aren't careful, the ashes will take you with them. I see blood around you as the devil takes your face, and it is either your heart or theirs. Cursed," she shivered and snarled at me.

That's not what my name means, I insisted, but now I wondered what my mother had seen...

Had she seen this moment?

It's their heart, mom, not mine.

I twisted my ring and smiled as I jabbed the needle into the black vein above her heart and dragged it down. Her eyes widened before something slammed into me, darting through the heart of the hive and towards the opening above.

"Indi," Chester yelled. "I've got her; we don't have much time before the hive reacts." He punched a krelin flying towards us and kicked another one as he hefted me on his shoulder. A jetpack of some sort was funneling the heated air and enhancing it for faster propulsion, and he could control the direction they aimed to guide them through the top of the mountain. He weaved out of the way of incoming warriors. I stared down his back and saw a limp green body hanging from threads, his head lulled against his chest, and I pushed and kicked out of Chester's hold.

He hadn't expected me to struggle, and he soared past me as my clothes expanded and helped me float to the platform Gaven was on.

Gaven, I repeated the name and felt my heart swell and heat. What the fuck was I doing? I landed hard on the platform as the hot air wasn't as strong directly above the ledge.

"I won't leave without him," I called out to Chester. The screech of the queen echoed below us, and curiosity had me looking down to see her trying to sink her fangs into Li-aq. I wasn't sure why they were trying to eat each other, but at least they were distracted.

I didn't have anything to cut Gaven from his bindings, and the needle on my ring had broken off in the queen's chest. Chester was working his way back to me, but the jetpack he had was designed to suck in the air and focus it; it would still be more difficult to go backwards unless he turned it off, which then was just another way of saying falling until he got close enough to turn it on again.

I jumped and got a bit of a lift to reach him dangling from above and clung onto him. The gust wasn't strong enough to lift us both when he wasn't wearing anything to help catch the air, and he was much heavier than I was. My face lifted to his jaw and adjusted his slumped head, but he was unconscious. He didn't even groan.

Chester caught up, and said, "We got to go. They are eating their own down there. It's chaos. I'm all about respecting different cultures, but I'll be glad when we get back to Estreldez."

"Do you have a knife?" I asked him with my hand outstretched.

"You know I do," he was calm even in this mess, and he turned on his jet pack to give it to me. I placed it against the thread and then looked at Chester.

"I need you to grab him. I'll use my clothes to make my way up."

"You're sure?" he paused to consider his own question. "Of course you are." He sighed with exasperation. "Yes, Boss."

"I'm not your boss," I chided. He was acting just like Bryce now.

"Whatever you say. We'd all be dead without you, so I guess this is the new crew member Indi talked about. Are you ever going to invite someone to the crew that doesn't owe their life to you?"

"Shut the fuck up and grab him before I cut this."

"Yes, boss," he said it again just to annoy me.

It still made me smile, and I cut the thick resin thread that held him up. Chester grunted as he hefted him on his shoulder and jumped from the ledge. The contraption on his back whirred to life with the inflow of the hot air, and he sped up towards the sky.

I jumped after I felt the wind strengthen and flapped my arms to aim for the next highest ledge to make my way up.

A krelin made their way straight towards me, and I gripped my knife tightly, ready to strike. He stopped just short, eying my hand and the glint of the metal. Li-aq...

"Queen Kai couldn't stop the black death from reaching her remaining heart. Take your mate and never return here. He will not be welcomed, even if we would have killed the nester ourselves. He took more lives than his." He took my hand and flew me higher towards the exit.

What was a nester?

He saw my confusion, and he averted his eyes towards the sky. "Desperation has led to many seeking self-interests. I will take care of it. I sense your ship has arrived." Then he let go of my hand, and I fell with a scream.

Air whooshed around me as I grunted from the impact of landing on something hard.

"Got her!" Bryce called out with a strained wheeze. "Close the hatch."

I pushed off Bryce and crawled over to the body strapped to the ground like cargo.

"You're welcome would have been nice to hear, boss."

"Didn't I warn you what would happen if you kept calling me boss?" I glared over at him.

He chuckled, "Sure thing... boss."

"Fucker, I cursed at him.

"For star's sake, you look like a death goddess after a massacre," Bryce said after a beat and wiped at his clothes like that would get the purple blood stains out, but it just smeared it around.

"More like a demon," Chester disagreed then pointed out I had horns on.

"Right... you're sure none of it is her blood?" Bryce asked.

It was Indi who replied through the ship intercom, "Minor injuries, she's merely in need of a lav sanitation."

Next thing I knew a puff of white powder was dumped on me, and I sneezed.

"What the fuck, Indi?"

It was decontamination protocol to have the powder absorb foreign liquids and neutralize any contaminations, but I didn't have to like it. Also, I would have preferred to clean up in the lav. What was worse was the powder was heating up on contact with my clothes, and I hadn't realized the whole entire garment was held together with krelin resin.

Piece by piece, the leather scales just fell from my body until I was sitting there in a pile of white dust like I'd played in flour... naked.

I wasn't ashamed of my body, but I was still a mess, just a different kind of mess now. Every one of my crew mates had already seen what I was working with, and none of them would be leering at me, but I wasn't going to hear the end of this.

Bryce sputtered and was the first one to laugh. "Boss," he teased me with the nickname again while adding, "you look like you got lost in a sugar vat!"

At least Chester would only make fun of me in his mind. I saw him smiling to the side, strapping himself into his seat after putting the jetpack away. Then he surprised me by saying, "She's had a rough few weeks waiting for us to rescue her; give her some space. You know sugar causes cavities."

"Right," he choked on his own rejuvenated laughter and said, "Right, sugar... cavities, priceless."

"Fuckers," I repeated but smiled to myself. They were horrible at making jokes, but I had a feeling they were doing this for me, not to me. I leaned over the unconscious green hunk and cupped his white dusted cheek to whisper, "You'll get used to them," as I teased about the grown children behind me.

As I felt the pull of breaking into Krelis atmosphere, I wondered out loud as I clung onto Gaven's body secured to the ship as it shuttered. "Do you think we could have done things differently? Or does fate really choose for us?"

Chapter
Nineteen
Ashley

The clothes weren't as comfortable as krelin-made leathers, but that was because their resin was breathable and secured the leather like a mold to my skin. They were extremely comfortable, but I'd found out more than once that the resin didn't stand up to estreld's radiation when concentrated, nor did it survive the decontamination powder.

While the clothing from Estreldez wasn't as soft as krelin leather, it did its job, more or less. Less was what they were used to... the pants they had on their ship were more like chaps in ancient farmer stories. They didn't have any covering for their crotches, which Indi said was because they had mating loh they preferred to have on display.

Even the shirt was basically full of holes everywhere for usual placement of their loh, allowing their jewels to absorb the moon's radiation. Did they even have nipples?

I blushed knowing they did because Gaven did. He hadn't worn a shirt when I met him. And the codpiece on his pants wasn't part of his clothes at all.

I cleared my throat. He still wasn't awake, even though the trip to Estreldez only took a few days. Estreldez gave us their fastest transport courtesy of the head of security, Hazel, and Indi said that she needed to see me immediately.

My fingers ran over the black slab of tarnpul that Gaven rested on. The healers said he was stable and he should have already been awake by now. The black stone was carved out like a shallow bowl, and it was filled with some nanotechnology jelly that should mend his broken loh.

"He should be dead," I heard one of the healers say when they thought I wasn't listening. I was always listening. Gaven's breathing was almost like a ghost's whisper, but I could hear it in my implant.

The medical team offered to fix my implant, but I refused. Not until I knew he was okay. Somehow, his implant was connected to mine, and I didn't want to jeopardize that, even if it meant not having access to all my coding backups. It felt vulnerable not being able to hack into anything, and my ring was broken, so I wouldn't be hacking into anything for a while.

Taking off my ring, I slipped it onto Gaven's pinky finger. "I'll be back."

The healer, dressed in a white robe that was practically see-through approached with a hesitant smile.

"In our culture, a female giving a male a token is a gesture of interest. When he wakes, he will know you care for him. I will stay with him while you are away," he offered.

The other healer chided him in a whisper, "It is unwise to encourage this. You know who he is." The female smiled tightly when she saw my glare.

"It doesn't matter who the fuck he is to you or your clan," I snipped. It only mattered who he was to me. Bitch, I grumbled under my breath.

She pressed her lips together and bristled while whispering to her colleague, "I'm only trying to protect her."

I didn't need her protection. I gnashed my teeth at her, and she flinched.

"Indi," I said, connecting to the wristband they had given me. They wouldn't allow Indi to go exploring on their planet, so he was confined to the ship orbiting the farthest moon.

I smiled at that. Gaven's offspring was named after the farthest moon, and his previous mate, Bina switched up to Nabi. All so that he could feel like she wasn't that far away at all. It was sweet. My hand instinctively went to my stomach, and my gut felt full of butterflies.

We were on the moon Lupa, where their best medical team was, used to vet incoming offworlders, and their security officer Hazel had just arrived through the moon shuttles.

"Mission Wizard was a success," he tried to convince me.

"Was it?" I asked sincerely as we left the lab and followed the glass hallway to the garden. A large, blue estreld with long white hair tied back was leading the way. He seemed to glow, and his jewels glistened.

The big blue alien didn't seem to be bothered with me talking to a voice he couldn't hear. The wristband was made to be more like an intercom, so he wasn't supposed to be able to connect with anything outside the device. But this was Indi, and he wasn't going to stay confined. He'd respect their privacy and stay out of their planet systems as long as we were safe, but it was easy for him to connect with my implant from a source so close.

"Success is objective," Indi said, and I was already sighing, hoping he wasn't about to go on some tangent. To the point, Indi, I moaned inside. We didn't have much time before we met with Hazel, Head of Security. I had a feeling she would have something to say about how Chester and Bryce had come to arrive on their planet.

"The queen of Krelis is dead, and that's one less worry for the power struggle of the planet," Indie began his list of positives, but even that positive was laced with darkness, "The estrelds have been fighting with that queen for independence. It was likely her survival would have resulted in another invasion attempt that would have succeeded in subjugating Estreldez with both Queen Mab and Prince Trent off to protect the sector from outlaws. The probabilities were high in that regard. The estreld forces are much smaller than the krelins. Their greatest defense is harnessing the radiation net surrounding their moons to disable and destroy enemy ships, but it's a defense that needs timing and preparation."

The estreld in front of me paused, and I could have sworn he was reacting in time to what we were talking about.

"Indi," I stopped him from continuing, "not to doubt your abilities but you did sweep the device you're on, didn't you?"

"The device does not have any coding other than to allow me communications through its speaker. I do have access to my servers through the ship. I've used it to connect with your implant, which is much too damaged to form any new connections. You're locked into the implant of your newest recruit."

I narrowed my eyes at the back of the estreld ahead of us. I didn't trust it. Something wasn't right.

"I heard a rumor when I was on Krelis that another human was with you, and she was taken. We'll have to return for her," I told Indi and knew the estreld could hear my side of the conversation.

"There was no other human with us," Indi said, making my face screw up in confusion. "An estreld was assigned with us on the mission, and we were told not to recover her after informing Estreldez of the situation. I had my suspicions that the ship was heading to Krelis regardless of our involvement. I detected an anomaly within the structure of the ship during our travels. It's likely more lifeforms were on the ship than were on the manifest."

I didn't care if the estreld I was following heard me say, "Fuckers used us to plant a team on Krelis."

I needed to test if Indi was being monitored without his knowledge, so I added, "Gho-ran will take care of it. Those damned horns connect directly with the hive; they probably heard everything we talked about on the ship."

"You sound as if you are happy that he would find the spies and handle them... I'm sensing that tone you use when you are--"

I cut him off before he spoiled my plan by saying I was bullshitting him. "It's not our problem, Indi." I used the tone he knew meant shut the fuck up.

I watched the estreld in front of us carefully, and he opened the door to the garden, which was a dome that felt like a hotbox similar to a greenhouse on Earth.

"If you'll excuse me, I have a communication from the farthest moon about possible outlaw sightings."

I smiled as he left, knowing he would never tell me "why" he was leaving if it had anything to do with an outlaw sighting. Fucker was bad at this spy business. They all were when they let their guard down; because I was being liberal with my words, he thought I was bad at this spy business.

He had been listening to everything. Probably going somewhere so he could tell someone to secure the horns I'd brought with us. His actions confirmed it because it was dumb to leave me alone, even if I was meeting up with another estreld in the garden. As soon as he was out of earshot, I whispered to Indi, "Code Zero."

"Understood," he acknowledged. Zero was the first incident we had come across when he had been infiltrated without realizing it. That time we lost all of those people, and he wasn't himself. He'd know it meant someone was listening and had access to his code.

A woman came out from behind a large rock covered in black flowers. "Clever," she said. "I'd expect nothing less from the Wizard."

"Head of Security..."

She was gorgeous, tall and covered in green jewels, similar to Gaven. The estrelds came in different colors, but most of them were blue and pink, some even purple. Green was a rare color on estreld, I had come to discover this after not seeing anyone green, excepting Gaven and now this lady. She had short, trimmed hair, and intense green eyes. She wore the lighter clothes typical of an estreld female, see-through gauzy fabric that flowed around her. Her eyes crinkled as she smiled and spoke of age and wisdom.

"Hazel is fine," she said kindly. "I apologize for sending you to Krelis, but they were looking for a prophecy, and I knew you would bring the queen out from hiding."

Was she saying what I thought she was saying?

"You sent me," I repeated that a few times over just to have it stick in my mind while I stared at her. She sat on the rock and plucked a flower, twirling it in her fingers.

"I can't do what you want me to do," she stated plainly. "I know you traveled far to help your species, but if you're here at all, that means the threat has traveled far."

"What are you saying?"

"I'm saying that the World Destroyer isn't destroying world s... it's protecting them. If I undo the virus, then the trill won't be able to keep this universe safe. I didn't create the Ganpan-Fal; I simply helped distribute it and stop it from being misused."

She was saying what I thought she was saying.

"Al-Hez..." Mother fucking... anagram.

Hazel.

"Your name is in the code," I insisted. She had to help reverse the outbreak.

"No," she corrected, "the name was there to seek out those with the skills capable of finding the name and finding me."

"You're a recruiter..." I surmised.

"In a manner of speaking, yes."

"So, you can't help fix the World Destroyer?"

"Not alone," she agreed, "but it's more than what you think. The World Destroyer isn't just a virus affecting fertility. It's a virus that prevents the replication of a species that's trying to root itself in our star system. If it succeeds, there won't be a universe to save. The World Destroyer is protecting us from invasion of the Solusgors. Without it, we don't stand a chance."

"You don't want to reverse the bio-weapon... you want to add to it..." I was catching up with what she was saying and trying to wrap my head around the fact that all this time I had been thinking finding her would solve everything. If she had created it, then she could uncreate it. But if Hazel was to be believed, then she hadn't created the problem; she was simply adding code to the original problem.

I felt my body slump and caught myself on the large rock beside me.

"Loric," Hazel began, "is listening as you suspected. He has been working with me for many cycles. I'm glad you reached out before allowing Indi to experiment with tampering with the virus. If he succeeds in neutralizing it, we would have more to worry about than the incoming war from outlaws."

"You're telling me Indi could have solved this without you?""

"Of course he could; given time and your direction, he could unravel the Ganpan-Fal, but you must convince him not to."

"Why should I?" I snarked. "You could just be blowing smoke up my ass and trying to stop us from undoing your bioweapon.

Don't think I don't know about how your code has also been used with biomarker tracking that has been used by outlaws across the universe."

"Because if you don't, we all die. The code was attached to the bioweapon to guide those that have the skills to reverse the Ganpan-Fal to this location.. I am not the original Starbreaker, nor will I be the last."

"You aren't even the one who placed the code..."

"No," she admitted. "It took many to create that code. The original Starbreaker was a commander of the Trillume Galactic Authority, a slave, a princess, and an underground civilization of a species who suffered the greatest destruction from the threat of Solungors, named after the broken civilization, themselves, for birthing it."

She sighed knowing pretty words would not be enough to convince me, and she also knew that killing me wouldn't prevent Indi from finishing the mission in my absence.

"I did not want to show you this," she began while my vision was taken over by a room of videos, surveillance of some kind of laboratory. "Indi can verify what you are watching is unaltered, and you may stop the feed with a simple command when you've seen enough to believe."

The species on the video were covered in strange glowing tattoos. Scientists moved around a body strapped to a table. His skin was peeling from his muscle and bone as he screamed. I winced, wanting to close my eyes, but the image was memorialized on my eye implant, closing my eyes didn't stop the scene, only made it darker like a veil had been draped over it.

Due to her hacking into my already damaged implant, it didn't pause when I blinked or tried to turn away.

"We lost him..." one of them said as the screaming ended with one final wheeze.

The video whizzed by on fast forward, bodies moving back and forth, and the dead guy was swallowed up by the table that was apparently set up to contain the body for further study later. I watched as a hand slammed against the clear cover where the dead body was. Blood smeared on the surface, and a scientist quickly came in and opened the table container up, calling out his name and then calling out to the other scientists on watch to let them know he was alive.

Only, he wasn't the same. The body clutched the scientist by the throat and snapped the neck at an odd angle. Then the zombie started to tear its own flesh off until... a completely different being was revealed underneath. It picked off the skin like it was a well-worn suit it had grown out of. I felt bile rise in my throat as the thing started to crack the other scientists' necks as they came in. The room was locked down to contain it, but the bodies that were left in there twitched, and the video fast forwarded again

The scientists that were prone and dead picked themselves up from the ground, and the strange creature licked and tore at the bodies to reveal... more of them.

Gray skin, black eyes, and they took on the forms of aliens they inhabited, but they were different now. One of them started to pull its teeth out, underneath which sharp jagged ones protruded from their black gums. I gagged, and it was Indi that spoke now, "There are many more of these videos of the same occurrence of an infected individual being overtaken by the invasive species. Do you wish to see the rest?"

"No," I gasped out. "Is it real?"

"I see no evidence of tampering beyond the sped-up timelines," Indi provided.

Fuck, I thought with defeat.

If this was what we were up against, then the Ganpan-Fal was child's play.

"You see why we can't neutralize the World Destroyer's code. It's the only thing preventing more of the Solungor breeding within us," Hazel explained. "The only thing we can do is keep distributing the nanobugs and hope one day someone can add on to the existing code to improve it. We work towards a cure that prevents the replication of the Solungor without affecting our own replication of offspring. No one knows where they came from or how to stop them from invading beyond preventing them from taking hold of this sector with the Ganpan-Fal."

"What can I do?" I asked through my rolling stomach. The image of those creatures coming out of those bodies would forever be emblazoned on my mind.

Chapter Twenty

Gaven

"Your mate is smart," a familiar voice said as I groaned. My head felt like it was pecked at by glorbin flighter thinking my loh were a snack. My hand reached up to hold my brain in its place, only to feel the cool touch of metal. I winced as I saw the grin of the Pride of Estreldez staring down at me. I was about to agree and say, of course my mate was smart, but if Loric was here, then...

Medical gelatin sloshed around me as I sat up on the tarnpul table. These weren't available outside of Estreldez. I narrowed my sights on Loric; then I felt myself spinning the new-found ring on my pinky finger. This was Ashley's ring. Had she given it to me? Or was this a parting token upon her death? My heart seized with both hope and grief mixed together, hope that this ring meant that she had accepted me as her mate and grief that it may be the only thing I had left of my Goddess.

"After all the missions we've done together, you still don't trust me. Understandable," he dismissed the slight of not acknowledging him beyond the momentary glare upon seeing his face, "You've had reason to mistrust me, and I've been a poor friend. With Luan's absence, I feel as if I've lost her, and it isn't the same, but it's been enlightening."

"Luan's disappearance has no comparison to Bina or Nabi's loss," I snapped.

He shook his head. "This wasn't how I wished to explain things to you."

"Explain what?" My hold over the pain ripping through my chest was slipping as I thought of waking without the sound of my mate's voice even if she were yelling at me, especially if she were yelling at me. I needed to know that she was safe... that she was alive. I couldn't bear to lose another piece of my shattered soul.

Many saw Loric and me as close, but the truth was that I didn't trust him any more than I trusted the Almder after what they had done to Mabel and the way he had looked at me with pity after losing Bina and Nabi.

"Do you think about what was done to Mabel?"

"Of course I do," I spat out. The pain in my head wasn't helping my mood, nor was the topic he had decided to bring up upon my waking. He would have done better to wait until I'd thoroughly fucked my mate and felt her in my arms. As it was, I was near to breaking, and if I didn't have my mate in sight soon, there would be bloodshed. I knew my implant was connected to hers; she should be hearing my voice, and I should be hearing hers.

"We don't have much time to discuss things. Please try to reserve your anger for me until the end. Your mate is currently speaking with Hazel in the gardens, and though she knew I was listening to her, she's not aware that I had need to speak with you without her present. She's been glued to you since arriving."

It warmed my heart to know that she was alive, and I trusted Hazel to not harm her. I visibly shuddered with the pent-up anxiety leaving my body.

"Speak," I said while swinging my legs out of the healing chamber. He was correct about one thing: there was little time because I would see my mate immediately. Nothing would satisfy me until I buried myself within her and felt her for myself.

"You left so suddenly with Mabel that I wasn't able to tell you or Mabel the reason behind the betrayal."

"I knew it," I growled out. He was just as culpable as the Almder in this mess. He lifted his hands in surrender, pleading for me to slow my thoughts to listen.

"I know you were paired with Bina for offspring and not out of anything more than obligations, but you should know that it was not your fault that she died. She knew what she was doing when she was asked to mate with you."

"Fuck, Loric," I rasped out. "Do you even hear your words?"

"I do, and you must hear me finish them."

"No, I mustn't," I said, pushing off the table and flaring my loh to test them and to burn off the slimy liquid stuck to my skin. It wasn't the first time I had been stuck in the healing chambers after a mission, but this was the first time I had somewhere important to be afterwards. I had to see my mate.

"She risked her life to test the cure for the Ganpan-Fal. If we could just cure the virus preventing our reproductive replication, the fertility crisis would be solved. Both of them died because they couldn't survive the Solungor virus. It had nothing to do with you. Almder prayed to the goddess for many moons to give you a family and to revitalize our clan with strong loh such as yours, but you were not compatible with any of our females. None of them triggered your mating loh, not until Bina had her virus neutralized. She was a strong enough match, and we thought miracles were possible because cycles had passed without any signs of her being harmed from not having the Ganpan-Fal within her."

I stared at him, speechless. He was saying Bina and my Nabi had been lost because they had a cure for the Ganpan-Fal... which made them susceptible to another threat. My fists flexed at my sides, ready to fight something, anything... anyone. Loric knew not to test me when I was in such a state. He remained seated across from me and then continued.

"I wish that was all," he said with a heavy sigh. "I didn't know everything about what they'd done to you or planned to do with Mabel."

I blinked at him, not following what he was saying, not wanting to follow what he was trying to tell me was more like it. He was, of course, talking about how I was no longer capable of providing offspring to my mate and how Mabel had almost had the same thing happen to her.

He stood then, and my arm loh formed sickled blades on instinct. I would be with my mate, or I would see his blood, and it was in both of our best interests if he allowed me to release my pain within the warmth of my mate and not in the warmth of his blood.

"Elder Ezra," that name made me grind my teeth in distaste, but Loric pressed on, "kept your fertile seed, just as she had intended to do for Mabel. But..."

Did I want to hear what he had to say? It took all of my restraint not to destroy the messenger of this information.

"If the huemoon is your mate—"

"It's human," I corrected him, and he gave a curt nod.

"If she is truly your mate, then your seed will take with her, regardless of the Ganpan-Fal's resistance to replication. Visit Elder Ezra when you're both ready. She isn't the enemy, Gaven. We are all victims of the Solungor. I hope to one day share the hope that is a true mate. I wish you both honored prosperity."

He ended his speech with a catch in his throat that made me believe he had stopped himself from continuing.

"Say it!" I demanded he stop keeping secrets from me.

"Before you're sent back out to defend our clan at my side, we can't wait for the outlaws to come to us. Warriors such as us must join our Almder at the front lines."

"Our Almder?"

"Luan," he verified my suspicions.

"What has happened to the Almder in my absence?" And by Almder, I meant Luan's lifebringer, and the one who had been Almder since before my time.

"The Almder is giving herself to the rock..." he said in a hushed but hardened tone. Did he not agree with this decision? "It is necessary to power the Red Wave to have someone control the netting. Anyone who triggers the radiation net around the moons will return to the rock. Even the clan must protect themselves from igniting the radiation waves when it's done. All ships around the moons will burn up, and only the moon god Lupa would be able to survive a surge of radiation so great to his loh, but the Almder will be able to stay alive long enough to aim the RW netting and protect the clan if necessary. We won't let it get to that point."

If he thought I would leave my mate, he was about to find out how wrong he was.

"Out of my way, Loric," I said while taking a step forward.

He didn't move. Determined to convince me, he pleaded, "The clan needs you, Skybender." He called me by the name of the monster the krelins believed I was.

"My life isn't mine to give," I told him as I pushed past. Without turning to face him, I added, "I've given it to my mate."

"Next time, don't be so fucking reckless with my property." A voice that had me shivering down my spine and warming my gut at the same glorious moment spoke in my mind. My mate, I thought with a devious grin. Where was she? The gardens, I remembered Loric saying something about her talking with Hazel. "You were almost eaten by krelins and apparently the only reason why you're alive is because you had something called glorbin flower in your system!"

If I had glorbin flower within me, then Li-aq had made good on his promise to procure it. She sounded agitated, but that would only make our mating more enjoyable as I made sure she knew I was not only alive but every part of me was hers. I would not leave her side again. There were other warriors capable of ridding the hives of the harvest nests. Other warriors could recruit to the cause of infiltrating the ships of outlaws, and others still could step up to defend the clan.

My life was for her now.

I had given enough to my clan, to my Almder, and even to the hive. They may not thank me for my efforts, but when I had killed those krelins, it was to save lives and help the hive clean up their mess so there could be peace between us. As for my

Almder, she tried to give me everything only to curse me with it. She had sacrificed Bina and my daughter Nabi for her own experiments. The only grace given was that Loric had allowed me the peace of knowing that my seed would not kill my mate and that my future still existed.

Finally, I spoke as I thundered through the halls, not caring about being stealthy or the following footfalls behind me. "My Goddess, I have much to atone for."

My mate rambled on about how she worried about whether I would wake up for several cycles during the journey to Es-treldez. As I approached the garden, she was running at the other end like a hergslat ready to thrash through rock to get to me. There were tears in her eyes as she ran that tore at my heart before I gathered her up in my arms. Her fists bashed into my chest, though they didn't hold much power in them as they dragged down more like a massage that had my mating loh heating.

"I don't care why you did it," she sobbed, "but if you break what's mine again, I'll kill you myself." She wasn't speaking of my breaking body; she spoke of what wasn't seen but felt. I knew this better than most. Losing Nabi and Bina had broken something in me that was only now piecing itself back together as I gripped her pounding fists in my hands. I lifted one to my lips and kissed it gently.

"I did it for all the victims he killed," I told her, not caring that Loric was behind us, listening. "The markings on his skin were a brand of every estreld he personally harvested for their loh. They were likely alive when being harvested. It was a mercy to end him quickly and a cleansing to their hive." I could feel the relief of having an explanation for why I had done what I had. The fight in her punches had already ebbed when I kissed each of her knuckles, but the tension in her shoulders didn't ease until she rested her forehead to my chest.

"Fuckers, I'll kill them myself," she gritted as she shook her head.

"The deed is already done," I assured her, and my other hand traced down her exposed back. I never found the clothing of my clan so alluring as I did while sensing all of her skin so bared to me. The top was not made for her specifically, and her nipples slipped between one of the cutouts of the leather made for the loh to have unfettered access to the moon's rays but served as unfettered access for my quickly heating flesh. I was wearing nothing, coming directly from the healing chamber.

"The universe is so fucked," she hissed out with despair, but she must have noticed what I had, as her nipples grew taunt and her chest rose and fell, rubbing them against my stomach.

I recalled the words she had said to me when I'd caught her in my arms last and repeated them back to her: "We have every fucking right to enjoy what we can from it before we return to the great rock." I was done repenting for my curse.

This whole fucking universe was cursed, and I would stop giving myself to its turmoil and instead worship the goddess in front of me. I lifted her up, and she wrapped her legs around me as I headed into the garden. Loric did not follow, and I heard him whisper his blessing in the wind, "In the moon's light."

In the moon's light, I thought, and as my mate's fingers wrapped around my neck, I felt as if she were the moon herself, washing me in her warmth.

"I wanted to be there when you woke," she confessed, and I smiled into her black curls, taking in her scent.

"You never left," I reminded her as I made my way through the rocks and foliage. Somehow, our implants were connected, and I wondered how much of my conversation with Loric she had heard. I hoped she wasn't thinking I would leave her to join Loric on a suicide mission onto King Sylve's ship. He had a whole crew of different species that wouldn't be as easy to stay undetected even with my cloaking ability. A groan escaped for more than having my mate wrapped around my waist. Why was I even thinking about whether they would find me sneaking on their ships or not? Once a spy, always a spy, I thought, but I wouldn't go anywhere without my Goddess.

One of her hands threaded through my hair, which had grown out a bit from when I left Estreldez, just enough for her to have a hold of me.

"I can't change the past, but I can give you my future," she rasped. Her breath was heavy as her nose nuzzled up against my chin and up across my cheek, and her lips grazed mine.

"Why forgive me, Goddess?" I hadn't courted her properly, and I'd put her in harm's way with my recklessness. Her forgiveness wouldn't change that I would never let her go, but it did bring peace to my molten soul. Now that I knew my seed was still saved with Elder Ezra, I wouldn't allow another male to be sired to her, and the thought of filling her with the very future she promised made my cock push against my mating loh's seam. It wouldn't be the last time I would seek her forgiveness, I knew. My mind was already racing with how I'd convince her to join me to leave this planet on the next ship out of here.

"Because you may have killed eight krelins in vengeance for lives lost, but I happily left an entire planet in turmoil just to make sure one estreld survived," she said with a shaking voice as she closed her eyes in shame. I didn't know everything she'd gone through while I was unconscious, but I knew that she'd done more for me than any living being in the universe would have for a blood thirsty male who'd selfishly killed eight instead of living to fight another day, to help protect her another day.

I stared at her for a moment in awe and worship before I claimed her mouth with mine.

Her fingers in my hair gripped tighter to pull my head towards her, and our lips battled for dominance, eliciting a heady groan from deep within me. My loh flared to life under her touch, but instead of forming weapons along my skin, they created a green glow that made the dew on the orange plants vining up the rock glisten and glimmer. The vine wasn't merely attached to the outside of the rock; I knew from experience that these vines were considered invasive if not tended to keep them controlled. They didn't just grow on rocks like moss; they rooted deep and could only have young sprouts pulled free from the surface. The rest of the vine would be part of the rock, and I thought it fitting that I should take my mate against such a plant.

That was what I would do to her, grow deep and become one with her to the point that to remove me would be to destroy us both.

"I would let the universe burn if it meant keeping you, Goddess."

"Goddess of the ashes," she chuckled before recapturing my mouth with hers.

Goddess of my ashen soul, I thought before I trailed my lips down her neck and plunged my fangs in. She gasped, throwing her head back against my hand so the rock wouldn't harm her. My other hand propped up her thigh on my hip, as she rubbed her wet cunt against my mating loh. I shivered with a growl. The small pull of her blood soaked into my gums and warmed straight down my throat, spreading through my body like lightning on the desert lands.

My loh on my thighs shot out and stabbed into the rockface, creating flat props for her legs to drape over, but I did not wish to be confined from being able to touch her. With a sadistic twist of thought, I released a knuckle loh into a sharp knife to cut the loh from my thighs while they were still forming and pliable; then I guided the edge of the loh up to curve and wrap around her thighs as they spread for me. The loh on my thighs being cut off made my skin burn, but I hadn't cut the root, so they'd grow back.

"What are you—"

I cut her off when I trailed my knuckles down her skin lightly until my face was directly in front of her beautiful cunt as she was suspended against the rock with the help of my severed loh. Her hands dug into my hair as she pushed against me to keep herself propped up where I needed her.

"Goddess," I traced a finger between her folds, and she bucked into the touch, and I growled. Whatever I was going to say was lost in my mind as I pressed my mouth into her giving flesh. My nose rubbed up and down, finding that bundle of pleasurable nerves that made her twitch with a moan. I wanted to bathe in her scent and devour every inch of her. My tongue lapped to taste her, and I became more thirsty for those noises and the pressure of her against me. I flicked my tongue up and down and swirled it around that hardened nub above the entrance to the afterlife of the gods. I sucked it into my mouth and loved the feel of it pulsing against my tongue too much to leave it alone, but I craved more of her taste.

Fingers rubbing at her entrance, I pushed two inside, easing it open to gather her essence. I felt the rhythm of her walls clamping down around my fingers, and my cock pushed out of my mating loh, eager to join in filling my mate. Scooping my fingers up to gather her taste made her shiver, and my motives changed directions once more. I licked up and down her cunt, tasting her as my fingers tried to find that spot that made her shiver again. Moving up and down with my fingers, stroking and sensing her reaction was greater each time my knuckles slammed to the hilt within her. I couldn't get deeper with my other fingers preventing the movement, but I moved faster, and she gripped my hair, tugging my mouth back to her clit.

Warm fluid filled my mouth as she screamed my name and her cunt squeezed around my fingers. "You fucking demon." She grunted as she bucked her hips. "Stop torturing me."

I grinned, licking my lips. "As you wish, My Goddess."

Every part of me was hers. I stood to line up my cock, rubbing it with her delicious molten heat. The first knot of my cock had already swelled from bringing her to pleasure on my face; it would be a tight fit, so I used my fingers to help notch it. One of her hands shot down to grab hold, unable to wait a second longer. She moaned as she worked my cock against her entrance and then let it slip along her folds, teasing over her clit and then back again. I took hold of her hand holding my cock and guided it within her, pushing over my first knot, both of us hissing with the sensation of her walls tightening around me.

"That's it; you take me so well," I said, stilling within her. It was a feeling like no other that had me closing my eyes and roaring with temporary insanity. It was like her body had said everything we wished to say to each other at that moment. I was hers, and she would never let me go. Don't ever let go, My Goddess.

Over that first knot half swollen, I felt the pull of her cunt as I sunk deeper. "Let me worship you as only a demon can, Goddess," I rasped as I thrust myself to fill her. Her whimper was all the approval I needed, and I felt my second cock slip within her folds, and I shivered as it ran across her clit, the sensation making me crazed. My second knot was swelling, seeking to stay within her perfect cunt that my cock was designed for.

She hooked her ankle into my ass and pulled me, adding resistance as our flesh slapped in an addictive harmony with her moans. I grunted as my hands explored her soft skin and found her mouth once more to devour that beautiful sound. Harder. I couldn't get close enough. Faster. My cock moved within her yielding flesh, and I reveled in the way her suction felt like it pulled to keep me close with each pull out to return to its home with more vigor than the time before.

My arms wrapped around her, and my head curled down to bury into her shoulder as I saw my death behind my eyes. My cock swelled within her and locked in as I thrust deep, hitting that spot I knew she liked as I bottomed out. Her screams muffled as she groaned into the top of my head. Body shivering, her arms and legs went lax as her spine arched. The waves of her cunt milking my cock made me shutter along with her. I cut through the loh keeping her suspended on the rock, both wrapped around her thighs like adornments, and I grinned to myself, loving the burn on my thighs that gave them to her and the warmth that coursed through me at being knotted within my mate.

"I accept your token, mate," I said while holding her close, my cock buried within her warmth.

Chapter Twenty-One
Ashley

Green loh were wrapped around my thighs like blown glass. His thighs were bleeding afterwards from giving them to me, but he seemed pleased with himself, and his thumb rubbed circles along my skin and traced where the loh met my flesh. What didn't make sense to me was that my own skin should be melting off my body with what I had been told about how estreld radiation worked, but no matter how brightly he burned for me, the only sweat I had was from panting at how thoroughly he fucked me into another realm.

The way he made my body sing for him, it was like his cock was made for me. I guess it was. We visited one of their elders called Ezra, and she explained an estreld's cock was nothing more than a resin that hardened when aroused. Most males could create a cock when mating, but until they found a compatible mate, their cock was literally just a hardened rod that gave pleasure but with no knots or pulsing fleshy feel from settling into its form. Fertile females were more common than fertile males, and that's why they opened the Mating Ceremony to offworlders.

Bryce was enjoying his time being "pampered" in the palace by fawning females. Chester still had a thing for one day being accepted into a necia tribe, so he didn't want to risk upsetting a female or male from the tribe with seeking a duel if his exploits created offspring.

Loric and Hazel had said the ship we used when fleeing Krelis was ours if we dropped Loric off somewhere. I wasn't dumb; I knew Loric was trying to recruit Gaven to help him on a mission. This was just his way of convincing him.

"You're sure?" Elder Ezra asked as she went to her BioStorage stashed in a compartment inside the wall that popped out with a wheezing suction sound.

I nodded.

"If you do this, it is common for an estreld male to lose themselves to their instincts when their loh finally sense the offspring in their mates. Even an estreld who is sired to a mate and has an offspring of another male have bonded to that offspring with ferocity. I don't normally dissuade from blessing the clan with another life, but you are planning on heading to Trillume, are you not? Perhaps, you should stay on Estreldez, where you both can be cared for."

"We have unfinished business to wrap up, but we plan on returning once we know you won't have to use the Red Wave. Gaven insists that staying on-planet is too risky for humans, even with our bond neutralizing the moon's radiation."

Elder Ezra shook her head. "We all seek shelter beyond the desert on the dark side of the planet, and we have other hybrids from human matings in our care. His concerns are unfounded, but I will not stop you."

"Don't tell him that I've taken a turkeybaster of his junk," I insisted, feeling awkward that I would be carrying around his offspring.

"I'm unsure of this tuukaybaste, but I assure you it isn't junk, and I've told you that he's made his demands quite clear that his seed was only to be used for you when you wished for it. His seed is yours to do with as you wish. I will keep the remaining essence here, but you may claim it at any time. Simply slip this depositor within your mating seam when you are ready. Hormones will be used to trigger your egg's release, and his seed will fill you. Give yourself at least one cycle of rest, allowing the depositor to do its job. No need to remove anything; the applicator slips out after injecting you, and the rest is a timed-release bio-seal."

A metal-looking tampon was handed to me, and I cradled it in my palm like it was the greatest treasure in the universe. To me and my mate... it was.

It was our future.

Gaven didn't know I was bringing it with us, but I wouldn't leave our child behind, even if it wasn't actually conceived yet. We had no way of protecting it if we were gone, and so I had to bring it with us.

"It's safe to travel with it?" I wanted to make sure I had all the necessary precautions to keep my family safe.

"The applicator is preserving it; just make sure to keep the device near a power source; it will charge automatically. The ship has power sources throughout, and it shouldn't matter where you keep it as long as the ship has power."

I nodded my understanding and quickly met up with the team at the port to load up into the shuttle and meet up with the ship.

Seeing Gaven standing there with his arms folded over his chest made me smile. I ran up to him and wrapped my arms around him tightly. He was pretending to be grumpy about Loric joining our trip, but I could tell it was mostly show. When it came down to it, we couldn't sit around and wait for chaos to reach us. We would face it head on, and there would always be a shit show to follow. There was never a "right" time to start our future in a universe fucked six ways to Sunday, and when we got out of stasis on the other side of the universe... I was going to have him slip his seed applicator into my needy cunt as he came inside of me. It may not be the most traditional way of starting a family, but I just thought it was right to have him inside me while I carried our future.

Then his keen green eyes looked down at me as I clung to him. Seeing the mischief in my own eyes, he grinned and captured my lips with his.

To our future, you glorious demon.

A whisper of words echoed in my implant, "To our future, My Goddess."

Author Note

Thank you for reading Her Alien Insurgent! The story of Gaven and Ashley was inspired by readers who said they really wanted to see Gaven have his own fated mate story, and though the reveals about the universe were set in stone, the fact that Gaven and Ashley were the ones to discover and unwrap those plot points was because of the enthusiasm of readers who wanted to have more of Gaven!

Your reviews, your ratings, your comments, and excitement for books helps fuel more books! So, thank you, and keep sending the love by leaving your own review/rating, sharing your love of the Trillume Universe to other alien lovers and let me know what you think of Her Alien Insurgent! Are you excited to read more in the Trillume Universe? Are there other characters you want to see more of? Your excitement and suggestions help fuel ideas and nudge me towards writing the next book as fast as my fingers can rub some words onto a page, so keep cheering!

Her Alien Starbreaker is the next book I'll be working on in the universe, with Hazel and Yuriel. And yes, every book is a standalone and can be read in any order, so delve into any of the other books in the Necia Warrior series or the Treasures of Trillume series for more alien romances! Her Alien Starbreaker is set to release within an anthology coming out December 2024, and then released with exclusive commissioned artwork in 2025, including a NSFW vellum insert! Get excited!

To follow along on what's coming, see teasers, progress, what I'm reading, exclusive goodies, or just say, "hi", join my newsletter and grab Her Alien Exchange for freesies, or join the Sky's Smut Between the Pages on Facebook! I hang out on Instagram more often than Twitter these days, so give me a follow: @authorsteviemarie

Thank you so much for being a fan of my alien romances, it means the world to my squishy heart.

Sky

Chapter
Twenty-Two

Starbreaker
Yuriel of the Trillume
Galactic Authority

M *any centuries ago on the rock known as Delta Fal*

Pulling into the desolate space junk that was a dead star with nothing but tradable goods to its name would be the only celebration my crew would have before we set off farther into the robe's edge of the sector not ravaged by the Solusgors. The chill of space made my scales flare up the sides of my head and I didn't have to say a word to Belder for her to know what was on my thoughts. It was on all of our minds.

"Will recruiting these volatile species to our ranks deter the Solusgors from invading?" Belder, my second in command, asked.

My jaw tightened with guilt. Even our queen knew it was not enough. History would not look kindly on my involvement in what would be needed to protect this galaxy. The cost would be high and should someone try to undo our efforts... death would come swiftly.

Could I live with myself for what I have done?

I would have to because at least we would all live.

I took a steady breath to answer her. "It isn't about whether they join us," I admitted.

"You think so? The threat that they might be could be enough?"

Involuntarily, I couldn't help my head shaking in the negative, revealing a truth I didn't want to burden her with.

"It will have to be. For now, we will celebrate the news that our queen has a fierce warrior planet joining our cause to protect this universe and all the planets within it."

The necia warriors were living weapons, and somehow our queen was able to use their own laws to convince them to join us. But having a show of force wouldn't be enough to stop the Solusgors. I only recently was given access to the records of what the threat truly was.

"I'm not sure how much celebrating we'll be doing on an outlaw planet that doesn't have any loyalties to Trillume..."

She had a point.

"This is our last stop before we return to Trillume, unless our orders change. It will still take many rotations before we see home again. Enjoy the change of scenery while you can, Belder."

"It is what is not seen that we must embrace in multitudes," she agreed with a bow of her head, seeking my forgiveness for not seeing the gift of having this small luxury before a long journey home. We had little supplies and what we gathered on this outlaw planet would be what we had to return with.

If we returned at all, I did not dare say out loud. The queen knew what she was asking of my crew and myself when she sent us. Our technology was great, but traveling this distance was still a gamble. If there were not enough supplies on this barren planet, there would be no return for us.

"Enjoy the time we have," I reiterated for both of our sakes. Belder swallowed deeply, the scales on her neck flexed with discomfort, and her green skin darkened at the small slice of skin peeking from her robes where she had undoubtably pulled at it seeking relief that wouldn't come from shedding the weight of our clothes.

I adjusted my own robes tighter around me and grunted as the confirmation of our ship docking at the planet's orbit station appeared on the display pannel.

It was time...

I flipped the switch on our cargo bays 7 and 8, releasing the bioweapon on an already barren planet filled with outlaws and unfortunate souls that were but a casualty of protecting the universe from the Solusgors.

They would live, the scientists assured me that its purpose was to stop the replication of the virus.

The Solusgors weren't a species as we pictured it, though that is what has been said about them to give them a form and something for our warriors and clan to feel like we can stand against them. A them to stand before, to unite against.

The warriors from necia were but a facade to make the planets under our care feel safe.

They would be safer, I thought with little amusement at what this would all cost us.

"Is it done?" Belder tore me from my dark thoughts.

I nodded, and my crew prepared to shuttle to the surface. Cargo bay seven was connected with our shuttle transports. Cargo bay eight connected with the docking station orbiting the planet... Every ship would carry the nanobots with them.

This would be the origin of what would be the deadliest attack on the entire universe, and I was the harbinger.

Belder didn't know the full extent of our mission, but she knew enough that what I just unleashed on this planet, on our crew, might mean we never made it home again.

Stay tuned on the next adventure, *Starbreaker*, within the Trillume Universe by joining Sky Robert's newsletter and grab Her Alien Exchange for free

SKY ROBERT

S.M. McCoy Writing as Sky Robert for Spicier Smuttier Romances

Sky Robert is a mom of two tiny humans in training, narrates audiobooks for fantasy/sci-fi indie authors, and when she isn't writing (which is MOST of the time) you can find her consuming copious amounts of coffee, promoting indie authors, reading alien smut, fantasy, sci-fi and romance books, chowing down on Indian butter chicken, and when she actually hangs out with people in person, in real life, outside of the internet (gasps), she's playing board or card games. All around nerd, lover of the strange, and all things fantastical.

More from the Treasures of Trillume Universe:
- ଔ Jewel of the Alien Bandit
  https://book.steviemarie.com/jotab
- ଔ Her Alien Prince
  https://book.steviemarie.com/heralienprince
- ଔ Her Alien Insurgent

Necia Alien Warriors: (Part of the Trillume Universe)
- ଔ Her Alien Exchange (Free)
  https://book.steviemarie.com/heralienexchange
- ଔ Her Alien Savior
  https://book.steviemarie.com/heraliensavior
- ଔ Her Alien Warrior
- ଔ https://books.steviemarie.com/heralienwarrior
- ଔ Her Alien Captor (Release TBA)

Also by S.M. McCoy

The slow-burn fantasy romances
https://linktr.ee/authorsteviemarie
www.steviemarie.com

Dark God Rising Series

ᙣ Taking Medusa (2023 N.N. Light Book Award Winner)
https://book.steviemarie.com/takingmedusa
ᙣ Breaking Fate
https://book.steviemarie.com/breakingfate
ᙣ Rending Olympus (Title Pending)

Her Alien Exchange

R ead this book for free and join my author newsletter:
https://dl.bookfunnel.com/f2fwrjww4p

She thought joining the alien exchange would only be for a year...

Violet

Human Exchange Trade, H.E.T., was my ticket off Earth. Leaving the planet to get away was probably an over correction and impulsive, but I needed a change. And what bigger change was there than to hop on a shuttle to a large spaceship that would take me to an alien host on the planet ASunGor for a year. I get to learn a new culture, fool around with a few hot aliens, and come back to Earth with a better perspective on my life. At least, that's what I thought, before I rushed the whole thing, and my host wasn't there to pick me up. Another exchange girl named Evie was heading to the planet Necias Prime looking terrified, and I had time to kill, so what harm was there in taking a detour to make sure she was okay? I mean, my reasons had nothing to do with the sexy alien that had come to escort her.

Commader Roe-el

I was reluctant to leave Princess Klemon's protection when she told me to escort a human to my home planet for a mating experiment, but in my haste to return to her side, I left without asking the name of the human. When I got to the station... there were two of them waiting, and one of them was making me regret not having tasted a female in years. Her scent did things to me, and I found myself going into rut when it was my job as commander to protect the humans, not screw them. Humans were much too fragile for a necia warrior, but the fire in her eyes made me question my priorities, and I couldn't say no when she boarded my ship. Everything inside of me needed to claim her, but she needed to say, yes, first.

Dive into a fated mates, spicy monster love romance with instalust, exhibitionism, strong female empowerment, alpha male with consent, and alien extremities. Join the fated mates of the alien warriors of Necias Prime in the Treasures of Trillume Universe. All stand-alone romances, within a fun interwoven plot of the universe.

VIOLET

As soon as the Human Exchange Training was open to the public, I was first in line to join. That might seem reckless, to immediately seek to abandon Earth for a year-long, alien-job training program, but anything was better than what I had going for me now. My ex was psychotic, and he didn't take my whole let's-be-friends conversation as well as I'd hoped. You really don't see all the red flags until the end. Sure, I was feeling uncomfortable with him for a few months now, but all that crazy made for great sex and had my mind all addled over the idea of leaving him simply because he seemed a bit clingy when I wanted to hang out with the girls. I had a decent job as a marketing consultant for what used to be the biggest IT company. But ever since we—meaning humans—were introduced to how big the galaxy was by these aliens called the Trill, well, our IT was way behind the times.

Too many people were more obsessed with the technology the aliens had to offer instead of what mere human mortals were working on. IT took a huge dive, and so did my career. I was a bartender now; that's how I met Mick... and he needed some time to cool off and find a new obsession. Living for a year with aliens while also getting training in a new career sounded like a win-win.

I left the recruitment center more excited than ever after being accepted by an alien host from some planet called ASunGor. It wasn't too far from the planet Trillume, which was where the trill were from. ASunGor was beautiful, with its purples, yellows, and oranges, and red gaseous clouds that, if they didn't tell me otherwise, I might have thought were poisonous. Red was usually associated with warnings, like my ex with all of his red flags. But I was assured the red was merely a reaction to the iron particles in the air hitting the oxygen, and the concentration was mostly in the atmosphere, not on the surface where there was a reasonable amount of breathable air for humans to survive without any harm.

I got a data packet about the aliens that lived there sent to my brain implant, which was updated with an alien language translator, so all that was left was to wait for the transport shuttle to take me to the ship waiting in Earth's orbit. I'd be gone for a year.

Before I could think on it more, I was interrupted by a cringe-worthy voice that was all too sickeningly familiar. Damn it. I had been so careful about getting here without being followed.

"What do you think you're doing, Violet?" he said from behind me, leaning against the brick wall of the recruitment center.

Clearing my throat, I jutted a hip out in defiance while replying, "None of your business, Mick."

He rubbed his gorgeous face with his hands in exasperation. That's what got me the first time around. Mick was too damned pretty, and I let that cloud my judgement for too long. The kind of sweet, chiseled pretty that made you think he was both adoring and capable of sinful things. And he certainly was capable of all sorts of sinful things that I used to look forward to—with relish—but it wasn't worth it.

"I know the IT industry has seen a dive, and you weren't looking to be a bartender your whole life, but offworlding? Come on, Violet, that's low; even for you. There have been plenty of news stories about how most of those aliens want to experiment with us, and a pretty girl like you... Violet, if you need a good fuck, you don't need to jump on a shuttle to find it," Mick said with equal parts disgust and interest. It was amazing how he could twist his words to both insult me and imply that his dick was good enough for the job, all at the same time.

I smiled sweetly at him, but anyone with eyes could see my derision as I retorted, "Oh, honey. I don't have to go anywhere for a good fuck. I've got myself covered just fine." I showed him my two favorite fingers and then lowered one to leave only the middle, silently saying 'Go fuck yourself' and ending with a little wink. It wasn't right to tease him. He liked it when I played hard to get, but I wasn't playing at anything this time. I was more than happy with my own company. Anything was better than the constant, back-handed compliments I received from him regularly. At least my own fingers knew my clit was bigger than just the tip that was visible. It was a whole fucking organ, and he wasn't its musician anymore.

Mick pushed off from the wall, and my whole body froze like a deer caught in headlights. I talked a big game, but the dark look in his eyes was terrifying and crazed. That same determined gaze used to make me smile, knowing we were about to have some great hate sex. But when I wanted it to end, the feelings changed, and he wasn't willing to let me go. I gulped back my fear as he slowly approached, but my feet wouldn't budge. His knuckles brushed against my cheek, and I instinctively pulled my face away before he harshly pinched my chin in his grasp to force me to look at him.

"You know you like it when that foul mouth of yours wraps around my cock before you scream my name. Your fingers can still do whatever they want when I'm fucking the sin from your dirty thoughts," he purred, pushing his mouth on to mine. My hands scrambled to find purchase, to shove him off, but he held me firm, and I struggled to slide my mouth away from his, gasping for air.

"Get off of me," I growled, and he released me at the same time as I shoved, making me stumble backwards and I lost my balance. He let me trip, falling to my ass, and he shook his head at me like I was a piece of trash that he'd have to pick up for the betterment of the world. I wiped his saliva from my cheek and forced myself to spit at his feet, to rid the taste of him from my tongue. "You're disgusting."

It wasn't that I didn't particularly like dirty talk; I did. But the way he said things was anything but endearing. It was possessive in a way that made my skin crawl. Like I needed to burn the clothes I was wearing to get the feeling of his hands groping me seared from my memory.

"No one will touch you the way you want it like I do, Violet. Not even an alien dick, if they even have one, would touch you after they found out what makes you scream," he threatened while licking his lips, trying to get me to think about all the things he wanted to do with his tongue. "Don't make me wait too long; this game of yours is getting old." Mick left me there sitting in what I now realized was a puddle left by the rain from the night before. It certainly wasn't my own juices that had soaked through my pants this time.

"Fucker," I gritted out, getting back to my feet and stomping back to the recruitment center. I opened the door a little more aggressively than I'd intended, but I was amped and pissed. Waiting for the later shuttle to "gather" my shit wasn't an option anymore. I was leaving tonight, even if I had to sign some extra waivers or agree to an extended exchange program. I didn't give a crap. I was leaving now!

Mick was lucky I ever touched his dick, and he was right. The game was getting old, but not the one he thought we were playing. I was sick and tired of him harassing me, and the authorities said there wasn't enough to get a restraining order. Not that it would have stopped him, I thought with disdain.

"Miss Thorn... did you forget something?" my recruiter, Beth, asked with a quirked brow at my now soaked pants and probably reddened face.

"Yes, I need you to get me on the next shuttle."

Beth pursed her lips as if I were insane. "You have no personal items with you. And usually people wish to say goodbye to their friends, family, someone before they go. You should really wait for the next shuttle in a few weeks," she insisted.

"No," I snapped before calming myself to reiterate in a less intimidating tone. "I want to leave on the one I overheard you saying was leaving today." I paused, then added, "Please." I forced a smile to my face and waited for her to deny me because what I was asking for was ridiculous. It was the most insane thing I'd ever asked of someone.

She lowered her voice and wrapped her arm around my shoulder to lead me away from the prying eyes of the other recruits in the lobby, eying me with concern. "Are you in trouble?"

I sighed, not wanting to get into this with practically a stranger, but she seemed so sweet and trustworthy, unlike my usual friends I hung out with. They were more encouraging of my bad choices. This was not a bad choice though, I reassured myself. This was crazy, but it wasn't a bad choice. As far as decisions went, sure, I should probably wait for my scheduled shuttle in a few weeks. But what did I have to lose besides a creepy ex and girlfriends that didn't even know a single thing about me, other than I was fun to have a drink with? Come to think of it, they probably mostly liked the cheap drinks I got for working at the bar... I shook my head. I was over the whole thing.

"I've got an ex stalking me, and a year away will be good for both of us," I admitted, but I didn't let her know that a sick part of me knew that if I didn't get on this shuttle, two weeks was a long time, and I didn't think I had the strength to resist Mick when he reflected on his actions in a day or two. He'd come back, sweeter than ever, and we'd have mind-blowing hate sex, and I'd hate myself even more for letting him get under my skin. I deserved better than what he was offering. I knew that in theory. But in practice... he was right. I was fucked up, and I liked how he made me feel when he wasn't being a petty asshole. He knew how I liked to be touched.

This was for me. I needed to recalibrate my brain and my body.

I didn't need his kind of possessive veneration.

"Yes, but you won't have time to go home and grab personal items. No matter how strong a person is, everyone gets Earth sick and misses the smallest of things that remind them of Earth when they are away." Beth was trying to talk me out of it, and she was doing a shitty job. I didn't give a crap if I missed the dirt or way pizza tasted. Sometimes, cold turkey was the best way to change your bad habits. I'd just keep myself busy to distract myself.

"Beth, I see what you're doing here, and it's sweet, really. But if you don't let me on that shuttle, my life is more screwed than if you let me leave. Trust me." I could see her lips press into a fine line as she led me through the building, probably to a holding cell because I was likely to harm one of us if they didn't board me on the shuttle today. I was that kind of desperate, and pretty much too angry to see reason beyond what I'd set my mind to.

She sighed in what I hoped was resignation, but it easily could have been her annoyance at another crazy she had to deal with in a diplomatic way.

"Violet." She used my first name, which was weird. "You have to be sure about this. The shuttle is boarding now. Once you're on, there is no coming back until your exchange is completed. Do you understand?"

Well, that was unexpected.

"Like, now, now?" My nerves were getting the better of me, and I was just as likely to bolt as I was to follow through with my hare-brained idea of jumping on a shuttle to a different planet.

She laughed, which was refreshing to hear, before she nodded her agreement.

This was happening.

I was leaving.

She was going to let me on the shuttle.

ROE-EL

The Princess of Trillume rolled her eyes at me, and I grumbled. Princess or not, she was asking me to do something that was akin to fucking an animal.

"My Princess, I think I misheard you. I apologize." I tried to show my disinterest without actually outright denying her orders of me. I was a reputable warrior, and I'd never questioned my position to be in her service, but this was too much. She must understand that if any other had asked this of me, I would have considered it an insult that would have been remedied by a duel before I agreed to anything more. Only if I failed would I submit myself to this. My upper lip snarled.

"You didn't mishear," she confirmed with a sly smile. "I need you to train a human in the ways of the Necia and encourage this human to attempt spawning with a Necia warrior. It's important to my research. I'm not asking you to be the warrior that attempts procreation with the human, Commander Roe-el. I'm asking you to escort the human to Necias Prime and train them before they arrive, while encouraging the human to be open-minded about your species."

"You're asking me to have another warrior," I paused to wrinkle my nose at the prospect, "spawn with a human. Do you have any idea what you're asking of any Necia you have do that? Humans are fragile, and deserving of our protection, but they are like pets to us that we've used as entertainment and companionship on long missions across the galaxies. They are NOT mates," I insisted with disgust.

Princess Klemon nodded. "I'm aware. They are not so barbaric to be considered animals, Commander Roe-el. They are just... different, and, according to my research, potentially compatible mates as well. You are assigned to go pick them up right about... well, now. You should head out if you are to get there on time. I know how you like to be punctual."

"Princess, my assignment is to you. Not your project. I would be derelict in my duties to leave—"

"Commander," she stopped me before I could finish. "The project is the reason why you are needed to protect me at all. If it makes you feel any better, I'll be sure to stay hidden in the lab until your return. You're the only one I trust to escort our exchange human to their new host. You won't be gone longer than a few weeks. There and back."

I narrowed my eyes, uncertain if I could trust her to stay within the lab walls while I was away and still grossed out by the idea of mating with a human.

With a huff, she added, "I'll stay put."

"I will not mate with a human," I clarified.

She shook her head in a manner that made me think she thought I was humorous, which made my shoulder epaulets twitch in agitation.

"I'm not asking you to be the one to mate with the human. I already have a willing warrior who is trustworthy and understands my research and what it means to the whole galaxy, not just Necias Prime," Princess Klemon explained, then did that hand motion she used to shoo me away from her research.

"Fine, but if I find that you have left this lab for whatever reason, you will be hard-pressed to have me leave your side in the future. Keep that in mind, should you get the desire to go exploring without protection." It was my job to make sure her family didn't find her and that anyone who knew what she was working on didn't find her. She was right; her research was too important to risk. If she thought I was needed to protect the human, then that is what I would do for her.

Arriving at the waystation, I grumbled, realizing Klemon had tricked me into thinking I was going to be late when I was actually early. Wasting my time waiting grated on my nerves like no other feeling. She was being cheeky when she said I preferred to be punctual, I knew that. I always arrived on time... never early. If I'm to be somewhere at a time, that is the time I arrive. No earlier, no later. On time.

And here I was, waiting like a fool for some human to disembark from their transport to Trillume and then reboard my shuttle to head out to Necias Prime. All the human exchanges came to Trillume first, then to their destinations. Never a direct route, as the humans were strictly monitored and accounted for. Couldn't have secret humans being stowed away and sold off in the markets. We'd never hear the end of it. There would be an open war between species about who had more rights to the humans and to Earth. The only good thing about that was I wouldn't be bored on my glorified babysitter duties of a princess. I might get a few duels in here and there.

The humans left the shuttle and appeared as I expected them to be: like scared animals, shifting uncomfortably around until a new owner came to take them to their temporary homes. One by one, they were being plucked away by ambassadors from various planets claiming their right to have their own human for a while. I realized I hadn't asked which one I should be acquiring for her highness' research. I mean, there wasn't much difference between them all, was there? Did it matter which one I brought with me?

I liked the look of the larger human that appeared to be less likely to be harmed by our Necia females. He would stand a chance of surviving Necias Prime with his muscles, though he still wasn't quite as bulky as I would have preferred to ensure his safety. I cursed under my breath, remembering that Klemon had said there was a warrior who'd agreed to mate with a human, and I hadn't asked if they were female or male. I waited a bit longer to see if another planet was claiming the human male. Shortly, I found out that someone had indeed chosen this male for their own exchange.

There were only two females left after the rush, and I found myself unable to remove my eyes from the one with bright red hair, the color of Necias's oceans. Unlike the other female, who appeared as frightened as I would expect of most who ventured so far from their habitats, this one folded her arms over her chest, highlighting small mounds that had my mouth quirking up in interest. I closed my eyes to rid myself of the thought.

Did humans possess some kind of lure not recorded in their data assessments? Not one warrior had ever spoke of this kind of attraction at the mere sight of the curves of a human's frame. Possibly it was my subconscious playing tricks on me after the discussion I'd had with Klemon. She had planted this idea of fucking with humans, and I had been without a female for some time because of my current assignment. It was difficult to acquire interest, or even spur on a rut, with a protective detail and not many options for duels. There had been no need to prove my strength and encourage my use of bed play.

But there that human was, and, when I opened my eyes, I was still enthralled by her curves and the strong stance of what I could only imagine was her annoyance at waiting there for her host. I blinked, regaining my composure. Waiting for me, I thought, and a sudden surge rippled through my body, sending a jolt to my cock. What on Horv's great vine was happening to me? This couldn't possibly be a rut, could it? Was I so far gone that merely the idea of mating and the mission back to Necias Prime had sent my body into rut? Had I waited so long in a boring assignment that my body found any excuse to claim and conquer even an animal such as this human?

I grimaced, but that didn't stop my eyes from watching as the female adjusted her hips to favor her other leg. Those silvery eyes of hers looked out in search of her alien host, and it was only her and the other female left. What kind of ambassador arrived late to pick up their human? Sure, I was making mine wait, but I was here. Surely the other host would know who they were supposed to pick up.

Wasting time was making my mind wander, and thinking of that human's small, fleshy mounds pressed against me instead of those small arms wasn't doing me any favors in improving my mood. I refused to rut with a human, it was an abuse of my strength to claim such a weak being in such a manner. Humans were helpless creatures that needed protecting, not warriors—or even broodmares—capable of taming a Necia warrior's epulknot in rut. I'm not a monster, I repeated to myself in an attempt to calm the hardening length down my thigh. I had to pick up Klemon's human before I decided to call this whole thing off. I'd just grab the human that didn't make me doubt my sanity and be done with it.

Approaching the females, I tried to move slowly as to not frighten them further, and the dark-haired female flinched and tugged at the other's arm in warning. It was wise for humans to fear a Necia warrior. This female had good instincts for self-preservation. We were predators in this ecosystem. And yet, years of evolution did not stop the other from lifting a brow and smirking at me in challenge.

"It's about time. I was wondering if I had to walk over and get you. Didn't anyone ever teach you that it's rude to keep a lady waiting?" she snapped off in succession. Her words stunned me momentarily as my translator had to catch up with the harsh, yet intriguing, sound of her voice. I towered over her stature and yet there she was, chin held firm as she stared me down. Those silvery eyes had flecks of gold, now that I was close enough to see it, and I could see her beneath me as I tried to count every star in her mesmerizing portals and plunged into her depths. My mouth salivated, and my cock pulsed, seeking a reprieve I could not grant it. This was too far, even for a rut-inflicted mind. I had to control myself.

She was a human.

Not some seductive warrior seeking sport on my epulknot.

Grab Her Alien Exchange for free

Her Alien Savior

Treasures of Trillume – Necia Warriors book one (Stand-alone-read in any order)– Available Now in Kindle Unlimited: Click here to borrow: https://books.steviemarie.com /heraliensavior

RILEY

Staring at the numbers highlighted on the screen above my head, I took in a breath and sat down. This was like any other job, I tried to convince myself. There was nothing left for me on Earth. Not anymore. With my brother gone, this wasn't just an opportunity to be adored by aliens while getting any kind of job placement training I could dream of. I took every course they offered to prepare humans for life outside of Earth, not that they were very thorough with much, but it wasn't about that for me. Learning a few new languages, basic self-defense courses, space travel 101, and of course a briefing on different alien species that are part of the exchange program was something to pass the time... distract myself.

My nails dug into my pants, creating indents in my thighs, unable to contain my nerves. Once my number came up, I'd be scanned, and my DNA would be paired with an alien host family. This was more than simply a job for me, this was something I had to do to ease the guilt burrowing deep into my soul, making my heart heavy and my veins thick with an invisible weight that would consume me over time.

"Number Alpha G, Lema U, Four Hundred and Sixty!" a male called out over the intercom system.

I was almost up; I'd been notified when my application was close to being chosen so I'd arrive on time. The room was filled with people, humans like me, hoping to be recruited into the exchange program. Being late could mean I'd have to submit my application all over again. Could I handle waiting a few more years of busy work? I'd taken every recruitment class they allowed me to, even learned an extra language besides the language of the trill. Cial was my favorite, because of the way it felt on my tongue to express the sounds needed to indicate a change in meaning of the same word. Many of the languages were only available for download to my implant if I was accepted by the host planet, but Trillix and Cial were part of an AI program to help get humans used to the exchange program and I taught myself the language with its help. I had a few years to burn waiting for my application to process.

Just think, an entire year of experiencing another culture, something new to learn, to distract myself. Maybe I'd like it so much that I would want to stay? It was better than most job opportunities on Earth, on file anyways, and I had to know that I didn't fuck things up, that I wasn't to blame for losing everything. Getting through a year in the exchange program would help convince me that I wasn't wrong, that I wasn't the reason my brother died.

"...Seventy!" they called out, distracting my dark thoughts.

I jumped up, lifting a hand. "Me!" I squealed, and the man beside me scrunched his brows up, like I was the alien in the room for being excited to be selected. You'd think he'd stare at some of the actual aliens that worked in reception with their scale-like skin and overly big eyes, and lack of hair. Not even the females from Trillume had hair, on their head or otherwise. There were only a few of them at the recruitment center today, and they wore masks over their faces because of something in Earth's oxygen that didn't agree with them. Only a few aliens were allowed on Earth, and even they were strictly monitored if they left the exchange buildings, and used some kind of cloaking device that made them look more human. They were usually only around when a shuttle was picking up exchanges.

The girl next to me shook her head at my fidgety nature and remarked, "You know the chance that you'll get to visit the Trillume Galactic placement center is like a fraction of a percentage."

That's where most everyone wanted to be accepted. It was the elite of all exchange programs. The aliens there were mostly humanoid, large, and sexy as sin. Most of the men in this room waiting for placement were none too secretly praying to be placed there because the females on Trillume were tall, voluptuous, and super into human men if they could make their way to the blue district, which was similar to the red districts of Earth where all the salacious happenings were allowed. Something about how powerful they felt in comparison to a human male, and how much trill women enjoyed looking after them. Almost as if humans were a kind of exotic pet. Very well-treated pets, but pets none the less.

I shrugged. Not my thing, but to each their own kink. No shame. I wasn't trying to mate with the aliens, I just wanted to learn everything I could about their technology and feel... useful. Feel like I was right about aliens, that what happened to my brother was just an accident and not some conspiracy theory. Losing him fucked me up in the head, and part of me thought doing this, seeing the aliens, would give me a small step towards healing and moving on, if only a little bit.

"It says here your name is Riley Spearit," the older man at the counter said with a wrinkled nose as he quirked a brow. It wasn't the first time someone had made fun of my name, but the derision was new.

"Yes." My voice lilted up, as if asking a question. Yes, it was my name resolutely, but the way he said it made me almost doubt my own name.

"Like a despondent spirit?" He wouldn't let it go. I sucked in a sigh, so I wouldn't appear ungrateful for even being here. Jobs were hard to come by, and the human exchange trade was no exception to that.

"No? But that does sound more creative than simply having parents that were really into this old singer from like the stone ages that was a king or something of rock music. Riley was his daughter," I rambled. "Also, it's not spirit, it's Spearit, like as in my ancestors way back when were warriors with spears and weapons." I was pretty good at spearing things myself, but I kept that to myself, it wasn't exactly an endearing quality to say I was good at handling a weapon that could skewer a person on the first greeting. They had my file, they would know I trained since a kid in weapon dancing. The art of handling weapons in a beautiful dance, but most didn't realize it was a legit martial arts that could disarm, defend and skewer if necessary.

"Right... Let's get this over with." He was not impressed and ushered me through the back towards the processing rooms, waved a pen over my body, then pressed it to my arm without any preamble, taking a DNA sample. It pinched quickly, and I flinched.

265

"Aren't you friendly," I mocked. He was not very happy about his job if this was how he treated all the applicants. I guess it was a long and busy career choice, constantly processing millions of people. Okay, it was probably trillions of people, all of them excited about space travel, the new frontier, learning about new species. I was no different.

Someone yelled, "No," from the waiting lounge I just came from. I looked over my shoulder, and another woman was ushered past us with her case handler whispering as they went.

"The shuttle is boarding now. Once you're on, there's no coming back until your exchange is completed. Do you understand?" she said while rubbing the woman's shoulders that were tensed up like she was going to fight someone. I knew what the tension of preparing to kick some ass looked like, and this girl was ready. I hoped the case worker could handle herself with that one.

"Like, now, now?" she squeaked, but after a few beats she squared her shoulders and they entered one of the rooms to speak in private. My own case worker swiped the air to transfer the exchange agreement to my implant, which displayed on my overlay viewer through my contacts that were provided as soon as I signed up to be part of the program. It was happening; I was so close to being assigned to an alien host family! The contract scrolled on for quite some time. I scanned the important bits, trying to quickly get to the end.

"Please sign this waiver," he droned, bored with his job, "We are not responsible should you have any adverse effects from joining the Human Exchange Trade—H.E.T.—or any dissatisfaction with your time, up to and including potential illness or death. You should know we take every precaution for every human's safety and have light years of advanced medicine to assist your success, but we can't account for everything. This is a note from the Trillume Galactic Empire, do you agree?"

The hosting species would never want anything bad to happen to a human in their care. It would destroy the trust built up over this exchange program. So, I wasn't worried about the double reassurance paragraph that made sure I read every word and forced me to sign that section alone before continuing to the overall agreement. It was important they made sure I acknowledged that space travel was dangerous, and they can't be held responsible if I decided to go against any regulations and eat something poisonous to humans or do something stupid and die. Because most aliens thought we were stupid, and humans were likely to harm their fragile bodies simply by existing.

I got it, our bodies weren't as resilient as alien ones. Whatever. I was tougher than I looked.

Signing the contract, I gave my guide a determined stare that I hoped said "Bring it on!" But it was just as likely that all he saw was a small human girl, dressed in a standard issue space leotard, about to face an adventure I'd cry about and insist on returning to Earth before my exchange duration was up.

Not happening, bucko!

A ding sounded in my ears, letting me know my application was completed.

"Right, so your information has been distributed with your personal data hidden until you've been accepted, then you accept the exchange offer. It can take—"

He's cut off when another notification grabs both of our attention. I was flagged for assignment... so quickly.

I was practically hyperventilating.

My guide stared at me, dazed for a moment, as if he was confused by it as much as I was, before he said, "Join me in the briefing room, Miss Spearit. My name is Joel, and I'll be your placement adviser for the time being." He seemed so thrilled to be stuck with me, the sarcasm was thick in my mind, but it wouldn't damper my mood.

"What does this mean?" I asked excitedly.

"It means there is an exchange opportunity posted and your data fits the request, so you'll be briefed. If you accept, then there is yet another approval process by the hosts to confirm your placement."

Joel was all of a sudden acting much sweeter towards me, and I'd take it. He led me to a conference room down the hall, behind the employee-only sliding doors that whooshed as I passed. The ground glowed yellow, then green—possibly making sure I was authorized to be there. I glanced around at all the pictures on the walls of other humans with their exchange hosts, some smiling and some not. There were a few exchanges not well-suited to humans, and those were flagged after people returned with their reports.

We were human advocates; not only did we learn, but we also helped bring back intel for Earth. It was a win-win.

I stared at one photo on the revolving screen display in particular. Which species was that? I mean sure I took a bunch of preparation courses for the exchange program, but though they provided different training for terrain survival, and trill culture from Trillume, they kept most information on a need-to-know basis. And if you weren't assigned to a species you weren't need to know. I read up on different species, and their uniforms made me think of the ones that were known as the alien police force.

"Those are the necia, a warrior species in alliance with the Trillume. They've been flagged as a bit too rough of an exchange for those on their first voyage. Only warriors are usually recruited—humans with talent in warfare, weaponry, and with exceptional strength. The necia make up most of the Trillume warrior fleets sent out to keep the peace between species in their system."

I cringed at that explanation. *Their* system, as if the Trillume owned all planets in this galaxy and the next several surrounding. I mean, they weren't completely wrong, it wasn't like anyone could stop them from invading any single planet if they decided to be dicks about it. Luckily for us, they seemed to be very diplomatic about everything, allowing humans to continue to manage our own planet with little interference.

"Don't worry, they don't assign females to their battle fleets, even if most of their missions are pretty boring considering no one wants to mess with the Trillume Galactic Law." He mistook my recoil at his explanation of the galaxy as not wishing to be assigned to the necia warriors. I'd never seen an actual necia warrior, or even a photo until now, but I'd read up on them, at least what they allowed us to know about them.

Suddenly, a stubbornness came over me that I was all too accustomed to, but Joel would probably baulk at. So what if I didn't have muscles like those necia warriors? The whole point of the exchange was to train and learn. I bet I'd be just as good of a warrior as any other human sent there.

"I checked 'all' on my application, so maybe I'll meet the necia one day," I replied casually. Necia were the warrior species that joined the alliance and became well-known as the enforcers of the galactic law. I knew that much, but I could see why their pictures weren't plastered everywhere like the trill were, and I smiled at how formidable they looked. They could strike fear into any human with spikes like that. Necia warriors were living weapons, and according to human laws, so was I.

"The females are quite aggressive... and territorial over their males. It's actually not uncommon for the necia females to be stronger. It's why mostly male humans are sent and not females... due to the likelihood of being killed in a duel for dominance. Their culture has, uh, tribal laws that the Tril-lume don't interfere with." Joel cleared his throat, and the room grew dark to highlight the display of a planet labeled AsunGor.

"It's beautiful." I gazed at the gaseous planet filled with bright colors. Where our oceans were blue and lands green and brown, theirs were a deep purple, yellow, and orange. Swirls of red clouds painted the atmosphere. Anything out-side of Earth was other and strangely captivating.

"ASunGor," he said with appreciation then quickly added, "but that was for a different assignment."

A new image appeared of a planet I was a bit more familiar with considering all the hype about the H.E.T. across all recruitment centers. Trillume.

It was massive compared to the size of Earth, making our sun's size seem normal at 109 times wider than Earth. It was no wonder Trillume was considered home to more species than the trill, becoming home to aliens that had lost their own planets, and making it the base of galactic law within any known star system, lumping Earth's galaxy into the fold of the Trillume Star System, T.S.S.

I stared in awe for a moment until the planet zoomed in and I got an overhead view of the main city, putting our own sci-fi movies to shame. There were quadrants creating habitats agree-able to many different species surrounding the city in domes that were created with forcefield nano nets that controlled every aspect of the environment without obstructing the view of the green sky.

Was I dreaming? Was I going to be given an assignment on Trillume?

"I'm only showing you this because something in your file was flagged, but I wouldn't get your hopes too high on this one. I've had plenty of flagged applicants be rejected once they've accepted the host."

"I'm confused, I selected 'all' under the training exchange. They should be expecting any human they choose to require training on whatever job they are offering..."

Joel sighed like this wasn't the first time he'd had to explain this. That didn't give me a bunch of warm fuzzies about my chances.

But this was Trillume we were talking about! No matter what my assignment was, it was the hub of many species, and on my off time I could explore everything. There was even a sexy, alien blue district palace if humans wanted to have some fun with no strings attached. I could only imagine the kind of kinks people discovered there.

Those necia alien warriors came to mind, and, though I wasn't a prude by any means, I wasn't really one to visit a sex palace either. Did the warriors even visit those kinds of places? They had to, right? They must get lonely after a long assignment patrolling the galaxy for law breakers.

I shook my head of the thought. I wasn't visiting an alien sex palace. I repeated that to myself, hoping that if I said it enough times, my curiosity wouldn't get the better of me. But all those hard muscles... the necia males didn't even wear shirts!

Joel cleared his throat to regain my attention. I smiled lamely, as if he couldn't see the blush on my face signaling exactly where my mind went.

"There is a scientist researching reproductive studies on various species that are on a population decline, and they have requested a human to assist their research biologically, but also intelligently. They will train on research basics, handling their technology, and evaluating results."

"Sounds important," I said, intrigued by the idea of helping another species. But biologically speaking, I'd be an awful specimen for child-rearing of humans. I couldn't have children, but damn if I wasn't going to help other aliens have theirs. Something deep inside of me ached, and I felt my eyes get scratchy. I quickly dismissed the thoughts of having a family and tried to refocus on distracting myself.

Choking back my emotion, I knew I had to get this assignment.

"You've been part of the other human's dismissals, right? Let's be real, Joel. What do you know?"

He squinted at me like I'd grown another head before he rubbed his temples. "I couldn't care less one way or the other if you get this placement, but I'll tell you what I know. It's become a bit of a running joke around the recruitment centers that a human gets flagged once a day for this job and not a single one gets through the final approval.

"But I wouldn't worry about it, having your file flagged even once makes you a more desirable candidate for placement. You'll get an assignment within a day of being dismissed. There is a whole sector of aliens that will only choose from the flagged humans."

"That seems odd, wouldn't it make us less desirable to be chosen and then dismissed?" I wondered out loud.

For the first time, Joel smiled and lowered his voice. "Between you and me, every alien has different preferences, and even being considered for a Trillume placement makes others want you more. And really, all the aliens are obsessed with humans; it's our government that regulates the H.E.T. and only allows a certain number of humans in and out. There is a strict no alien exchange in place until Earth is more comfortable that their laws would be followed, and no invasions like sci-fi horror stories would occur."

I nodded. That made sense. There was probably a limit to how many humans were allowed to leave at any given time to any given planet. So Trillume was the most sought-after placement, and there weren't many accepted. Could that be caused by humans deciding to stay in their placements longer than the exchange year?

The aliens that were in the reception area from Trillume were probably strictly monitored and only part of the exchange agreement to oversee the process.

"Do you know how many humans are allowed on Trillume per the treaty agreement?"

Joel shrugged. "They don't release that kind of information to the public, or even the recruitment centers. The trill probably know, but they don't talk to us much."

So, he didn't know, or he wasn't going to tell me. I guess we weren't all that chummy since he'd first decided on a single glance that I wasn't worth his time. But someone on Trillume thought differently. This was my chance to finally have a new start.

To finish what my brother started.

DIREL

Being considered for advancement was everything I was waiting for. No more endless cycles drifting through space on the off chance of finding some idiot breaking Trillume Galactic Law. As much as I respected the Trillume way of allowing planets to run their own business, it only took one act of disrespect for them to turn feral and make you wish you'd listened the first time.

They'd send our best warriors to remind them what respect and honor meant.

I smiled at the thought, that was why my planet assimilated with them. They challenged our king and won. They were a worthy warrior to serve, and our king abandoned our planet like a coward, creating his new home on a barren land surviving on imports, trade, and from the rumors circulating about Necias Delta Fal... the alliances of outlaws.

This was the last mission before my promotion to less remote assignments. I'd served from the beginning, and I knew this was all a test of my honor to assure the council of my tribe's intentions to comply with the treaty. Huffing out my exhaustion, we docked at the industrial epicenter of Necias Delta Fal. Meeting with Sylve was like having my failures stare back at me across the hall.

Had I tried harder to convince him to stay, to fight for our tribe, would things have been different? Betrayal still sat heavy in my chest, both my hearts strained even seeing his face. He'd chopped off his hair short the day he left, a sign of leaving our tribe and everything he stood for.

"Vox Direl, it's a pleasure to have you visit Necias," Sylve said through tight teeth, still sore about me not joining him in his exile. I was his second, and I could not follow his path when it would lead to the death of our tribe. We had to bide our time, understand what we were up against, and yet he chose to create a new planet for himself instead of lead the one he left.

"It's Commander Direl," I corrected. My epul shoulder bones stayed on display signaling I didn't consider him my king, or deserving of my respect. This was not a social call, this was business. And this wasn't Necias Prime, this was a barren parasite of a planet, surviving solely on imports, and dark trade. Even if I did withdraw my spikes, they would still show to some degree. My bones had grown too large to comfortably store them under my first skin as I once did. A sure sign of my leadership, and power.

Sylve still sported his spikes around the crown of his head peeking out from his shortened silver hair... Silver strands laced through all necia warriors, but his was consumed with it. It was not a sign of age. Once, I had thought of his coloring as a sign from the goddess that he would lead our tribe to many victories. He had, for a time.

"Commander, then. You were always one of my strongest *male* warriors."

I grimaced hearing the emphasis on 'male'. It was a slight he knew I'd pick up on. Not even the strongest of male warriors, just one of them, and pointedly remarking on the fact that any female warrior would have been considered stronger. Fine, if he wanted to be petty, then perhaps, I'd find some time to have a proper duel while I was here. My fists clenched and I tried to calm myself.

The gleam in Sylve's eyes nearly undid me. He knew how to get under my skin, he was like a brother to me before he left.

"You always did have a temper," he dismissed, leading me to his command center for this planet. "I have an assignment for you, Commander Direl."

"I don't take orders from you," I grunted, recovering my senses. Something made my skin burn like the call to battle, toughening my scales around my forearms, thickening my dermis in preparation for danger.

"Oh," Sylve quirked a brow and turned his back to me, "That wasn't an order. This is a demand, in response to having complete control over your battle vessel."

Now, I was the one at a loss for words as he continued walking ahead of me. There was no way he could have seized control of my ship. I took every precaution of leaving command to my second, Chuel, and explicit instructions not to disembark until things were secure.

"Without my authorization codes, I hardly think that's a very intimidating threat," I tried to call his bluff, but something in my very bones told me something was amiss.

"You see," he continued as if I said nothing, "I have need of your Trillume-marked vessel. No one would dare interrupt its travels, and there's been reports of a species that is compatible with all sorts of biology that could be the answer to my current troubles."

"You're going to have more trouble than you can handle if you're planning on disrespecting the courtesy given by the Trillume to manage your own business. They will crawl so far up your ass there won't be another planet that would touch you."

"Such feisty threats, but see, the Trillume already plan on shoving their unmentionables up this whole sector's ass if I don't do something about it. That's why you're here, or didn't they tell you? No? That's a shame. They must not trust you enough to tell you that the moment you place that data core into my command station to 'check' on my dealings, they would seize complete control over this planet, and use your forces to keep a foot hold here until more of your fleets arrive."

He had to be lying, how would he be able to know a plan I wasn't even aware of. What exactly was in this sector that they cared enough about to invade? They already owned this star system. These planets already paid a tithe from their exports.

"I can see you're having trouble digesting this information." Sylve appeared thoughtful, and even sympathetic as he sighed. "I'm glad it's you, brother. Perhaps I can talk some sense into you. The Trillume aren't the reasonable warriors you think they are. They take what they want, and they've destroyed entire planets that didn't bend to their will."

"They are, by our own tribal laws, ruler of our tribes. They did not destroy our planet, and our warriors live as they have always lived. Our tribal laws are respected," I tried to reason with someone I considered a friend once, family even.

"Direl... Do not be blind. They used our own laws to their benefit, and other planets that don't submit willingly as we did were not so lucky. Entire species nearly extinct, even some by our own hands under the control of Trillume. Wake up. Or be forced to see them for what they are in a less than honorable way."

I didn't understand, there was no way he would best me at a duel... and I felt myself stumble across the causeway, the infinite darkness of space surrounding us with the only illumination beneath our feet lighting our way.

When? I thought with alarm.

Sylve turned to peel off some latex third skin from his hand. *No...*

"You'll be fine in an hour. It was a steep trade to find the elder root from Necias Prime, but I'm not a monster like the one you currently follow. I wanted to do this in a civil manner. Don't worry, I'll regain both of our honor by dueling you properly when the time is right. See you in a few weeks, brother."

"What did you do?" My voice gravelly from induced sleep. The elder root was a home remedy for warriors in rut without their mate. It was the only kindness we could give them to shut down the body before the chemicals took over our minds. But it only lasted an hour if not reapplied to a warrior not in the heat of rut, and Sylve had said weeks...

"I'm putting you in the stasis pod until we reach Earth. Don't worry, I'll explain more later. You'll come to understand I did what was necessary."

This didn't explain how he had control of my vessel, I thought as my mind went foggy. The only explanation was betrayal. My second... Chuel followed our old king...

And I should have seen this coming after what we'd lost together.

Continue reading Treasures of Trillume – Necia Warriors book one (Standalone-read in any order)– Available Now in Kindle Unlimited: Click here to borrow:

https://books.steviemarie.com/heraliensavior

Want More?

For more information about upcoming books in the Treasures of Trillume or Necia Warrior Series (or any other books by Sky Robert) like me on Facebook or subscribe to my newsletter.

Thanks for reading! You are a book hero!

All the squishies,

Sky

xoxo

www.ingramcontent.com/pod-product-compliance
Lightning Source LLC
Chambersburg PA
CBHW070557260626
47161CB00002B/628